THE ATTIC

THE ATTIC
DANILO KIŠ
TRANSLATED AND WITH
AN INTRODUCTION
BY JOHN K. COX

DALKEY ARCHIVE PRESS
CHAMPAIGN / DUBLIN / LONDON

Originally published in Serbian as *Mansarda: satirična poema* by Kosmos, Belgrade, 1962; an earlier version of this translation first appeared as *Mansarda*, published in a limited edition by Serbian Review Press, 2008

Mansarda by Danilo Kiš © Danilo Kiš Estate

Revised translation and introduction copyright © 2012 by John K. Cox
First edition, 2012

Library of Congress Cataloging-in-Publication Data

Kiš, Danilo, 1935-1989.
[Mansarda. English]
The attic / Danilo Kiš ; translated and with an introduction by John K. Cox. -- 1st ed.
    p. cm.
"Originally published in Serbian as Mansarda: satiricna poema by Kosmos, Belgrade, 1962"--T.p. verso.
Includes bibliographical references.
ISBN 978-1-56478-734-7 (pbk.)
I. Cox, John K., 1964- II. Title.
PG1419.21.I8M313 2012
891.8'2354--dc23
                        2012015155

This translation has been published with the financial report of the Serbian Ministry of Culture

Partially funded by a grant from the Illinois Arts Council, a state agency

www.dalkeyarchive.com

Cover: design and composition by Mikhail Iliatov

CONTENTS

TRANSLATOR'S INTRODUCTION

Danilo Kiš was born on February 22, 1935 in the northern Serbian city of Subotica. This city, known in Hungarian as Szabadka, has long been a crossroads of cultures; it lies in the northern part of the region known as Vojvodina, on the great plains that characterize central Hungary and lap over into eastern Croatia and western Transylvania as well. It has been a polyglot border town since the end of the Habsburg Empire in 1918. In Subotica and throughout the Vojvodina one would have noted in the interwar period the presence of Slovak, Ruthenian, German, Jewish, and Croatian minorities as well as the larger Hungarian and Serbian populations. This region, arguably the most diverse in all of the former Yugoslavia, was also home to two small, little-known population groups: the Šokci and the more numerous Bunjevci, who are Roman Catholic by tradition and are generally held, on the basis of their dialects, to be Slavic (possibly Croatian) settlers from points south and east.

Kiš's father was named Eduard Kiš, a Hungarian Jew who worked for the Yugoslav railway company. Kiš's mother, born Milica Dragićević, was a Montenegrin Serb by nationality and an Orthodox Christian by religious affiliation. Eduard died in the Holocaust in 1944. Kiš and his mother and sister spent the war in Hungary, returning to Montenegro in Titoist Yugoslavia in 1947. Kiš went to school in Cetinje and university in Belgrade. He taught at several universities in France in the 1960s and 1970s. After defending his works and his approach to the art of writing in several rounds of literary and political polemics within Yugoslavia, he took up more or less permanent residence in France in the 1980s. He won several significant literary awards during his life, and passed away on October 15, 1989. He is buried in Belgrade.

Yugoslavia's lifespan in the twentieth century encompassed all the major developments in European history from the end of World War I to the end of the Cold War and the fall of the Berlin Wall. The country existed as a (variously defined) union of six constituent republics from 1918 to 1991, and Kiš's life fell squarely into the heart of this time period. Royal Yugoslavia had a troubled existence before the Second World War, and the wartime experiences of Kiš's family personally, as well as his country as a whole—foreign occupation, the Holocaust, a brutal civil war—represented a sharp escalation of those troubles. The second, or socialist, Yugoslavia also began with a time of considerable pain and violence, as the communist leader Josip Broz Tito settled accounts with ideological foes and potential oppositionists through massacres, purges, and stifling cultural and political policies.

By the mid-1950s, however, Yugoslavia had evolved to a new stage, and it was in a much different cultural milieu that Kiš started his literary career. Belgrade had always been the metropole of South Slavic culture; one can assert this without disparaging the significant cultural achievements of other cities in the region, such as Zagreb, Sarajevo, and Ljubljana, which lacked Belgrade's broad-shouldered bluster and the intellectual autonomy that came with political independence. Belgrade was first the capital of the independent state of Serbia and then of both Yugoslavias.

Belgrade was recovering from the various atrocities visited upon it first by Nazi and then communist rule by the time Kiš wrote his first novel, *Mansarda* (which, translated here as *The Attic*, might also be titled *The Garret* or *The Loft* in English). And, at least as importantly, Yugoslavia too was recovering. After Tito's epoch-making split with Stalin in 1948, Yugoslavia developed its own "third path" of maverick socialism that soon left the arts a considerable amount of room to maneuver. By 1960, the hidebound dictates of socialist realism were largely dead; artistic controversies did still crop up, often fueled by inter-republican rivalry and sometimes by the lingering taboo on criticism of Marshal Tito and the reputation of his anti-Nazi guerrilla forces, the Partisans, but Kiš was basically free to experiment with pan-European trends, taking his place beside older and internationally recognized Serbian writers, such as Ivo Andrić, the 1961 Nobel laureate in literature, as well as the important voices from his own generation, such as Antonije Isaković and Borislav Pekić.

READING *THE ATTIC*

The Attic is the delightful story of a Belgrade bohemian nicknamed Orpheus. He is a writer and a lute player, a skirt-chaser and a philosopher, a dreamer and—probably—a perpetual student. The novel is set, rather vaguely, in the capital and coastal regions of Yugoslavia in the 1950s. As he is wrestling with his feelings for a young woman he calls Eurydice, Orpheus is also wrestling with his calling as an artist. Towering over Orpheus's actual comings and goings and his not inconsiderable flights of fancy are the colossal, perpetual, neon-lit questions about ART: What is its relation to reality, and how should a person's commitment to it affect his or her personal life?

Like Kiš's other prose works, *The Attic* is not complex in syntax or diction. But it does contain more humor than his other novels—humor that reminds one of his (as yet untranslated) short stories such as "An American Tale" or essays such as "Shakespeare and Sausages." We come across a skeptical goldsmith in Chapter One, a lewd but erudite blotch of mold on the ceiling in Chapter Two, a riff on the perils of amateur translation in Chapter Three, an unusual payment in kind for English lessons proffered to the "sluts of the port" in Chapter Six, and so on. Indeed the entire book is shot through with wordplay manifested in nicknames and permutations on designations for food and drink and other consumer products. There are brief but bracing love scenes, the light decadence of barroom shenanigans, an encounter with a prostitute, and a lot of trading in stock literary and pop-culture references. Underscoring the youthful feel of the work—youthful for the protagonist as well as his real-life author—are the compendia of "big questions" and food for thought in the first two chapters. These are the issues, indeed, that teenagers and twenty-somethings in all cultures have to spend their time sorting out and, one hopes, answering.

Orpheus lives in an attic with Billy Wiseass (real name: Igor) in a large apartment building in Belgrade. The two young men philosophize and read and party and decorate their apartment in in the way of young, irrepressible intellectuals and city-dwellers.

They are, in fact, coming to terms with "the meaning of life" and awakening (in the manner of one of those coming-of-age novels that literary critics call a *Bildungsroman*) to life's possibilities and limitations and costs. Orpheus meets a young woman he really likes. He then takes off on an imaginary (or real?) trip to the South Seas where he gains new perspectives on courtship and European identity. He senses that he is walled in by his own egocentric perspectives and that *writing* about *other* people might prove to be his liberation. But he has a long row to hoe.

By Chapter Four, Orpheus is back in Belgrade, where we are treated to a dose of postmodernist discourse from the cleaning lady, who has fallen in thrall to Billy. But so has another, younger woman, whose accidental pregnancy serves to illustrate another strange dilemma of the postmodern writer. Kiš, it seems, just can't leave the controls of meta-narration alone, for we then go skimming along a lengthy pastiche of Thomas Mann's *The Magic Mountain*. Orpheus continues to be plagued by a real tension between art and love and also by a glaring inability to nail down his actual or proper role in managing either.

Always in search of new "takes" on reality, Orpheus and Billy open a pub and continue their meandering ways. Their decadence is really just sloppy self-discovery. Their indulgence becomes tempered by encounters with their emotional and physical limitations and their artistic needs. A great mystery or puzzle of life, perhaps *the* Ultimate Dilemma for the idealistic and the naive, is posed at the end of Chapter Seven and then again in the following chapter. Should one compromise with life? Or is it better to kill oneself than give in to "reality"? It is the same rigor and passion in Orpheus that makes it hard for him to decide between these two options that also makes it necessary for him to compromise with life. The reason for this is that his art will never find space to develop if he remains rigid and self-centered; his appetites will consume him if he adheres to a false consistency.

Then, in another bar with another friend, we find out that Orpheus is writing this story (in the form of a novel with the same title as the book we are reading) as he's living it. Our unusual and rather casual hero finally takes note of the mottled variety of life around him—especially the misery of some of his neighbors in the apartment building. Images of girlish innocence and fragility at the end of the book hearken back to the early chapters, and Orpheus is ready for his new mission: he decides to "dismount from this star" and start to meet the world as it really is. He knows he can expect a rough ride, as the closing scene conveys to him. The same thing applies to Kiš himself, for whom the writing of this book can be seen as a kind of exercise in the development of an artistic credo. It is a blend of autobiography and mission statement.

One of the best summations of Kiš's style of writing is made by the American scholar Ilan Stavans, who notes that Kiš was "hyperdescriptive" in the manner of Bruno Schulz and "concise and astonishingly erudite" in the manner of Jorge Luis Borges.[1]

The Attic itself is the work of a young author. This is obvious not just because of its date of publication but because it is, to quote

1. Ilan Stavans, "Introduction to 'Dogs and Books' by Danilo Kiš," *The Oxford Book of Jewish Stories* (New York: Oxford University Press, 1990): 325.

the Austrian critic Karl-Markus Gauß, "a brash and tumultuous work" in which the author "demonstrates his jaunty reverence for the bohemian world" and "his rigorous ethic of detail."[2] This latter characteristic would prove enormously important in Kiš's later work, as would the nascent elements of postmodernism in *The Attic*.[3] The Serbian critic Petar Pijanović has studied extensively the "quest for form" in the novel—that is, the meta-narration involving the blended character of Orpheus, who is both narrator and author.[4] Form is obviously something that Kiš was studying for himself through the writing of this work.

Reviewers and critics writing for English-speaking readers have barely commented on *The Attic*, since it has not been available in English until recently. But, in the eyes of this translator, the novel reads as a powerful statement of Kiš's nascent artistic credo at a crucial time in his artistic development. That is to say, it is difficult to ignore *The Attic*'s apparent reflection of many contemporaneous developments in the author's own life: the biographical elements of a bohemian *Bildungsroman* are quite prominent. A young storyteller at the time, a Balkan bard like his protagonist, Kiš too was finding his voice and formulating his credo, which is ultimately rooted in a strong sense of connectedness to other people. Some of Kiš's hallmark stylistic traits—such as the lists of

---

2. Karl-Markus Gauß, "Auf dem Grunde des Pannonischen Meeres: Danilo Kiš," *Die Vernichtung Mitteleuropas: Essays* (Klagenfurt: Wieser, 1991): 128–129:

3. Jovan Delić, *Kroz prozu Danila Kiša* (Beograd: BIGZ, 1997): 38.

4. Petar Pijanović, *Proza Danila Kiša* (Priština: Jedinstvo, 1992): 69.

realia, the learned (if miniature) digressions, the ironic humor—are already present in *The Attic*, although the crushing weight of history that envelops his later prose is absent. Rich in references to music, painting, philosophy, and gastronomy, as well as literature, *The Attic* is a laboratory of technique and the anvil of an artistic ethos—and, of course, a more than self-assured first novel in its own right. As a work of art, *The Attic* is at once a depiction of life in bohemian Belgrade, a register of stylistic devices and themes that would recur throughout Kiš's oeuvre, and an account of one young man's quest to work out his approach to representation by balancing art, life, and text. Whether or not we read it as a "portrait of the artist as a young man," *The Attic* adds up to an admirable first novel, indeed.

This translation is dedicated to the best set of language teachers a young American could have had: Frau Fritsche, Marilyn Jenkins Turbeville, Kim Vivian, Roger Weinstein, Magda Gerő, Sibelan Forrester, Anto Knežević, Piotr Drozdowski, Anka Blatnik, and Jana Kobav. Thank you!

And thanks are due too to Milo Yelesiyevich, my first editor on this volume, whose input and aid were invaluable to the project.

JOHN K. COX, 2012

THE ATTIC:
A SATIRICAL POEM

We will not catch sight of any romantic cell, cabin, or thatched-roof hut; before us will rise a multi-story stone edifice; the higher the floor, the colder it is to live there. Poverty, sorrows, misfortunes, ignorance, and illness drive a person higher, up one floor after another. While a person is down below, he or she is still interested in the colorful jumble of life and participates in it in some fashion, even though it has generally been incomprehensible and inaccessible to him since birth. (With the rise of civilization the number of people "maladjusted to life" grows—one should not lose sight of that fact.) The more that life pushes a person up to greater and greater heights, the colder it gets for him or her, and the less one is capable of comprehending life and adjusting to it.

— A.A. BLOK

EURYDICE

I listened to invisible trains weeping in the night and to crackly leaves latching onto the hard, frozen earth with their fingernails.

Everywhere packs of ravenous, scraggly dogs came out to meet us. They appeared out of dark doorways and squeezed through narrow openings in the fences. They would accompany us mutely in large packs. But from time to time they would raise their somber, sad eyes to look at us. They had some sort of strange respect for our noiseless steps, for our embraces.

Some heavy blue autumn plums dropped onto the path from a shadowy tree whose branches jutted over a fence. I had never believed that such firm blue plums could exist in autumn. But back then we were so preoccupied with our embraces that we didn't pay any attention to things like that. And then one night, in a startling flash from the headlights of an old-fashioned car, we noticed that a band of dogs, which had so far followed us silently, was gathering plums, almost reverentially, from the gravelly road and the muddy ditch. All at once it became clear to me why the dogs were so silent and dejected: these wild autumn plums had contracted their vocal cords, as alum would. I heard only the pits, with which they were allaying their hunger, cracking between their teeth. It looked, however, as if they themselves were ashamed of all this; as soon as the car cast the unexpected illumination of its headlights, they hid in the ditch next to the road, though the ones who hadn't had time to get out of the way remained stock still, as if petrified.

Then the car stopped all of a sudden and out came a man in a sheepskin coat.

"Strange," he said, but I couldn't see to whom he addressed these words. I couldn't tell if there was anyone else in the vehicle because the light wasn't on.

The man in the sheepskin squatted next to the dog carcasses and contemplated them for a long time, repeating the words "Strange! Strange!"

We flattened ourselves against a cracked old wall in the shadows and held our breath. The only other thing we saw was the man getting back into his car and switching the headlights back on.

It was only when the automobile was already moving down the road that the engine roared to life. That's when it dawned on me how the man in the sheepskin coat had managed to take the dogs by surprise. The car had been rolling down the road with no lights, in neutral, with the cunning of a wild animal; and the wind was blowing in the opposite direction.

Then we jumped over the ditch and halted at the spot where the car had stood just a moment before. Both of the dogs lay on their right sides, almost symmetrically arranged next to each other. One of them was an old bulldog with a simian snout that the tires had mutilated; the other was a small Pekinese with a medallion around its neck. I stooped down to look at its collar. The following words were stamped into the yellow medallion, no bigger than a fingernail:

—*Larron. Crimen amoris.*—

I hoped that I'd find a notice in the newspaper, that I'd be able to make a statement and give the medallion back to the dog's owner, but I was never able to find anyone advertising for his return.

Therefore I took the medallion to a goldsmith one day, after I'd convinced myself that there was no reason not to consider this piece of gold my personal property.

"*Larron* means swindler," said the goldsmith without looking up at me.

I was astonished.

"That was my dog's name," I said to conceal my embarrassment.

"Strange!" he remarked.

"He liked to steal plums."

"Plums?" said the goldsmith, looking up at me.

"It cost him his life," I said.

"Strange," he said. "And you want me to make you a ring out of this?"

"Yes," I said.

"Hmmmm," said he. "Of course, that's your business."

Then I said, "You mean you really can't make a ring out of it."

In those days I didn't pay any attention to trains. But they tormented me with their screams without my even being conscious of it. Some kind of dark presentiment grew in me, a dread of their howling.

Nonetheless I said one evening, to my own surprise, "I'm afraid of trains."

"You aren't afraid of anything," she said. "You don't need to be scared."

"I'm also afraid of dogs," I said.

"Oh!" she said, but she was unable to say anything more. The moment she had rounded her mouth to say "oh," I glued my lips to hers, so that our kiss intoned a dark note of repentance, a hollow, protracted "oh . . . oh . . . oh . . ." which swelled up and thinned until it burst with a light pop, like a bubble.

"Oh!" she repeated, and now her voice was huskier, more intoxicated.

"What's wrong with you tonight?" she said.

"I shouldn't have said that. You shouldn't have permitted me to say it."

"What?" she asked.

"That thing about the trains and the dogs. I shouldn't have verbalized that. If I hadn't mentioned it, I wouldn't be thinking about it now."

We lay in the dry leaves next to the railway embankment.

I have never been able to explain what goes on inside me. As soon as I sense, from a slight rumbling of the ground, that a train is approaching, I am overcome by my masculine instincts and some sort of anxiety, agitation, which compels me to dash under the wheels.

"Hold me," I said. "Tight."

"Are you frightened again?" she asked. "There aren't any dogs here. Or did you hear something?"

"Yes," I said. "The cracking of pits between their eye-teeth."

"That's the watchman making his rounds."

"No," I said. "Just hold me tight."

As the train thundered past, making a whirlwind of the withered foliage that we had thrown together in a pile, I trembled, on the verge of fainting. Then, suddenly and inexplicably, I began to sob.

"Take a look!" she said. "Look!"

It was dark enough that I didn't need to blush. Furthermore, I wasn't even ashamed of crying. I thought about coming up with an explanation for her, but I gave up on that too. I even liked the fact that I had cried in front of her.

"Look here, you lunatic!" she repeated. "Look what I found." Only then did I open my eyes.

She was holding a blonde rag doll in the palm of her hand. I took hold of its chintz dress with two fingers, pulled up its little skirt, and laughed out loud.

"This is our baby," I said. "Immaculate conception."

"You're making fun of me," she said.

"No, I'm not."

"Good," she said. "Let's baptize her."

"No," I said. "Let's toss her under a train. She has a snout like that bulldog that the car ran over."

She looked at the doll's face for a moment, then gave a small cry and flung her, spinning, over the embankment.

I felt nothing but the sawdust from the doll's guts coating my face like sand.

"Strange," she said, when she had torn herself away from my lips.

"Yes," I said. "What's strange?"

She lay on her back in the withered leaves, staring up at the dark night sky.

But all the stuff between us had started a long time before that.

Back at the time I think I first met her, I was feverishly demanding answers from life, and so I was completely caught up in myself—that is, caught up in the vital issues of existence.

Here are some of the questions to which I was seeking answers:

—the immortality of the soul
—the immortality of sex
—immaculate conception
—motherhood
—fatherhood
—the fatherland
—cosmopolitanism
—the issue of the organic exchange of matter and
—the issue of nourishment
—metempsychosis
—life on other planets and
—out in space
—the age of the earth

—the difference between culture and civilization
—the race issue
—apoliticism or *engagement*
—kindness or heedlessness
—Superman or Everyman
—idealism or materialism
—Don Quixote or Sancho Panza
—Hamlet or Don Juan
—pessimism or optimism
—death or suicide
and so on and so forth.

These problems and a dozen more like them stood before me like an army of moody and taciturn sphinxes. And so, right when I had reached issue number nine—the issue of nourishment—after having solved the first eight problems in one fashion or another, the last addition to the list turned up: the question of love . . .

Broken down into its component parts, this issue had—in a concrete case—the following determinants:

Question: What color are her eyes?

Hypotheses: Green, blue, blue-green, the color of ripe olives, aquamarine, like the evening skies over the Adriatic, over Madagascar, over Odessa, over Celebes; like the sea at Brač, at the Cape of Good Hope, etc.

Question: The color of her hair?

Hypotheses: Brown, blonde, like fairy hair, hair like the Lady of the Lake's, the color of mellow moonlight, of pure sunny flax, of a sunny day . . .

Her voice?

The voice of a silver harp, of a viola with a mute, of a Renaissance lute, the voice of a Swedish guitar with thirteen strings, of Gothic organs or a miniature harpsichord, of a violin staccato or a guitar arpeggio in a minor key.

Her hands, her caresses?

Her kisses?

Breasts, thighs, hips?

So, this is how she came striding up to me, with this precious baroque burden, with the gait of a tame beast of prey and the wind in her hair.

It was like this:

It was right when I—along with Billy Wiseass—wanted to dedicate myself to philosophy, and we had without much effort just arrived at that famous ninth problem, when he proposed that we skip it, since it was pretty vulgar and of no interest to real philosophers, and instead dedicate ourselves to astronomy and begin that whole business about the stars and planets.

Naturally I agreed.

To this end we sold all our things (that is to say, his coat and mine, and several books that we had wrung out like lemons and thus could have tossed into schoolhouse urinals anyway) and moved into a *mansarda*, a small attic loft on the outskirts of the city. There we gaped at the stars day after day, or rather night after night, and discovered several galaxies we had never before heard about or seen. We christened one star from the constellation of

Orion "Undiscovered Love," and a second one "Billy Wiseass," and a third star we christened with my name (let's let that stay a little secret), and a fourth we named in a straightforward and pretty vulgar manner: Hunger.

In this way we justified our inconsistency and our return to the grand and unworthy question bearing the cabalistic number 9.

"Allow me," I said, "to introduce my friend to you: Billy Wiseass."

"Oh," she remarked. "You must surely be a philosopher."

"No," I said. "He's an astronomer."

"Yes," Billy Wiseass said, "and he's a—"

"—globetrotter," I interrupted, aiming for his rawest nerve. (I've never liked to bare my true nature in public.)

"Oh," she replied and her eyes skimmed across a cloud.

"Yes," I said. "I've just returned from the Cape of Good Hope by way of the Côte d'Azur."

"Lucky you!" she said.

"Lucky us?" I asked.

"Lucky us," said Billy Wiseass.

The autumn of the year 7464 (according to the Byzantine calendar) was foggy and wet, yet the foliage turned yellow and dried up overnight, so that one morning I was astonished to discover that the branches were as naked as pipes. All of this occurred so unexpectedly!

"So what's your name, actually?" she asked the next day. "I assume it's not 'Cape of Good Hope.'"

"Orphée," I said. "Orpheus."

Billy Consummate Liar confirmed it:

"Look here, Magdalena," he said. "Why shouldn't you be called Eurydice? He undoubtedly meant to suggest that next . . . Right, Orpheus?"

"Of course," I said. "That goes without saying. If you have no objection."

"Oh," she said. "How strange you are!"

Then, a surprise attack:

"So where's your guitar, Orpheus?"

"In the attic," I said.

"Which attic?" she asked.

"We live there because of its proximity to the stars. You understand. We will rename 'Hunger'. . . 'Eurydice.' Do you like that idea?"

"I don't get it," she said.

"In order for one star at least to bear your name."

"My name isn't Magdalena."

"Who said anything about Magdalena? I said 'Eurydice.'"

"Oh," she said. "I don't care. But I would like to see this star."

"Certainly," I said. "We will select a star that is worthy of your name."

ATTIC (I)

The next day I led her up the dark wooden stairs to the attic. I had already chased Billy Wiseass out, and I explained away his absence by expressing my amazement that he wasn't around.

"That's not nice of him," I said.

"It's not," she agreed.

"Maybe he left to go to the observatory," I said in his defense.

"But where is your guitar?" she asked, casting a glance around the room.

The room resembled the hold of one of those small sailboats pitching back and forth on the high seas, lost in the dark of night. On the walls the dampness had sketched out wondrous designs of the flora and fauna that bloom and thrive only in dreams. On the ceiling was a depiction of the birth of the world from the embrace of dewy sleep and tentative wakefulness, while in the four corners stood symbolic illustrations of the four continents: the African summer, the Asian spring, the snows of America, European autumn.

Mastodons and reptiles grazed on the walls, and hummingbirds plucked thick mucus from the eyelashes of a woolly mammoth. Flocks of wild doves (the last examples of which were to be found in this attic) and cranes and swallows covered the walls, forming an enormous wedge in the shape of the numeral *1*, thereby providing an illustration of biblical brotherhood and the mythical marvel of friendship: *And the swallow will build its nest in the ear of the mastodon, and the hummingbird will comb the leopard's mane with its silvery beak, and the woodpecker will clean the teeth of the crocodiles of Niagara and the Holy Nile.* (The Gospel according to Billy Wiseass, translated into Mansardic from the Galactic and rendered in verse by ———, known as Orphée or Orpheus.)

With our fingernails we had copied out Latin and Greek maxims all over the wall (wherever it didn't detract from the pictures drawn by the hand of dampness). We abided by them like the Ten Commandments and, in times of intellectual crisis and despair, we recited them like prayers of purification. They were guideposts to truth, *lux in tenebris*, as Billy Wiseass said. Who else would have hit upon the notion that people needed to carve maxims into the wall *ad unguem*, "by means of their very fingernails, until the blood spurts."

Here are some bits of wisdom from the Temple of the Attic:

Jos arta, caci se prostituat!

*

Quod non est in actis (in artis!) non est in mundo.

*

16

Plenus venter non studet libenter.
*
Nulla dies sine linea.
*
Abyssus abyssum invocat.
*
Nec vivere carmina possunt.
*
Quae scribuntur aquae potoribus.
*
Ho bios brakhus, hê de tekhnê macra.
*
Castigat ridendo mores.
*
Amo, ergo sum.
*
Credo quia absurdum.
*
Tempora si fuerint nubila, solus eris.
*
Felix qui potuit rerum cognoscere causas.
*
Gnohti saeuton.
*
Habent sua fata libelli.
*
Os homini sublime dedit.
*

Pectus est quod disertos facit.

*

Albo lapillo notare diem.

*

Mens agitat molem . . .

Do you recall, Billy Wiseass, the cry:
—*O ubi campi!*
And that wise teaching we did not wish to follow:
—*Primum vivere, deinde philosophari!*
And this example of arrogance:
—*Hic tandem stetimus nobis ubi defuit orbis.*
(Here we finally stand, a place that has fled our earth.)
Oh, that attic!

On the floor there was grimy straw that had been strewn about and trampled; it was teeming with roaches, so that in the middle of the gray day (the window was plugged up with rags and faded old newspapers) you could hear the straw rustling beneath their tiny feet. We had placed our books on the bed and wrapped them in diapers of cellophane, but even there the rats found them and so we had to keep the most important copies under a bell jar weighted down with a rock. Billy Wiseass had swiped the glass cover from The Three Elephants for this purpose; he had simply clapped it down over his head and announced to all the folks there: "With this I shall travel to the stars." Everybody (including the waiter) laughed at this joke, so witty, and given his age, so ambitious. Under this bell jar we stored the following books: Spinoza's *Ethics* in Latin, the Holy Scriptures in Hebrew, *Don Quixote*, the *Communist Manifesto* by Marx and Engels, Breton's *Second Manifesto*, a *Handbook of Diet Foods*, *Pensées d'un biologiste* by Jean Rostand, *Yoga for Everyone*, Jeans's book on the stars, Rimbaud's *A Season in Hell*, Stendhal's *On Love*, Weininger's *Sex and Character*, reproductions of Van Gogh prints in a pocket edition, and an international train timetable.

Our clothes were hung on hooks in the ceiling, exactly in the middle, where Venus's vagina was to be found, having been sketched in there, in the shape of a shell and seaweed, by the marvelous imagination of the dampness. On these hooks protruding from Venus's flesh were suspended Billy's black velvet pants and my black ties, of which I had in those days approximately two hundred. On another peg hung a nylon bag in which we kept our toothbrushes, shoe polish, pomade, and shaving supplies. In one corner or in the middle of the room (it actually had no definite location) there was an old-fashioned rocking chair, with an already unraveling wicker seat, which stood us in good stead for philosophical conversations and daydreams. Whichever one of us was running amok at the moment used to rock in that creaking chair and utter Pythian prophecies and visions. A dull, cracked mirror hung a bit crookedly above the washbasin, which was made of the most diaphanous Chinese porcelain and reverberated with every word like a seashell.

"It isn't actually a guitar," I said.

"It's not a guitar?"

"It's a Renaissance lute," I said. "You're probably wondering . . ."

"Oh!" she said, alarmed. "Something is crawling up my leg."

"It's nothing," I said. "A mouse, for sure."

"A mouse?!"

"Well, what else could it be? The snake's already asleep."

"Oh, God!"

"It's over there, under the bell-jar by the books. We extracted all the poison from it. I brought it back from Ceylon," I noted with pride.

"And what do you want with a snake?" she asked.

"Are you familiar with the legend of Orpheus? Of course you must know it."

"He tamed wild animals with his songs," she said, trembling.

I continued:

> *The boulders opened their portals before him, and the Andes and Cordilleras bent their ears to hear.*

"So where is this thing of yours, this . . . Renaissance guitar?"

"Lute," I corrected her.

"Okay, then. Lute."

Then I opened the rusty little door for cleaning soot out of the stove, and a swarm of squeaking mice and rats came hurtling out.

She leapt onto the bed.

"Now, Eurydice, you are going to hear the song of Orpheus," I said and struck up a tender arpeggio in a minor key.

I sang softly:

> *A rose petal your pillow will be,*
> *and tulips your footsteps will mourn.*

She sat with her legs folded beneath her and watched me—with fright or with amazement, I don't know.

Then she said: "Look! Look!"

"Eurydice," I said with pathos in my voice. "You can stretch out your legs."

She was staring, dumbfounded, at the little iron door. With the dignity and discipline of ants or worker bees, a column of cockroaches was climbing up the wall toward the opening. They waited for the last mouse tail to be yanked in before continuing.

When the final bug had made its way up the wall, I clapped the iron door shut with my foot and started singing:

A rose petal your pillow will be,
and tulips your footsteps will mourn.

"Not now," she said. "Not now, please."

(That must have been later. At least one light-year later. I believe that the light from the star named Eurydice—which I caught sight of at that moment—set out on its journey on the day that I first beheld Eurydice, and I believe that her "no" at this moment meant that we needed to wait until the light of that encounter had reached us.)

"Fine," I said. "The light has to ripen."

"What kind of light?" she asked.

I explained it to her.

"How will we recognize it?" she asked.

"The summer declination will show up in your eyes. Can you imagine? Like when olives ripen overnight. It will be beautiful," I said.

"Oh," she said.

Suddenly her eyes grew dim, and dark pollen covered her lashes. The lute fell with a bang into the thin straw. It emitted a mellow

21

chord of a type no one had ever heard. As though the fingers of twilight had strummed the strings.

Nothing could be further removed from my immediate ambitions than to write a romance novel. Although I feel that the whole business starts somewhere around there, after the caresses. I don't want to make a tea set. I want to make crystal, as the wonderful Billy Wiseass would put it. That poor bastard has it good: he's never experienced love. It'll be easy for him to write a romance novel. If only he would give up stargazing. Nonetheless, Billy Wiseass, you will admit: it's too cold out there amid the galaxies.

Or do you disagree?

When I sensed that I had pushed things too far, I said to her: "I have to go away. To Uganda. To Tanganyika. To Equatorial Africa. It doesn't matter where. Far away."

"Take me with you," she said.

"What are you thinking. Dearest. My one and only."

"Why are you lying?" she asked reproachfully.

"I swear!" I said. "Do you want me to prove it to you?"

"How?" she asked. "How?"

"I won't leave."

"Oh, that's nice."

"I'll kill myself," I continued.

She looked into my eyes. "If those are your only choices, then go. You *must* leave on your journey."

So, my dear Billy Wiseass, for several light-years I was absent, ailing. I hope you won't have changed so much since we last saw each other that you will be capable of asking me why I left, why I fled.

But you see, I have changed. I've become feeble-minded and several light-years older (I didn't say wiser). And, as you can see, I'm posing this question to myself: Why? Why?

Wiseass, do you remember our vows in the attic? Our sage pronouncements? I'm ashamed that I let myself ask the question *why*. Did we not say: when you go too far, think of crystal and run away?

But that was all such a long time ago!

Personal experience in such matters is irreplaceable.

Do you recall, Billy Wiseass, how we wanted to become murderers just so that we could enrich ourselves by the experience? The problems started (do you remember?) when we figured out— you had already prepared the pistols—that if we acquired the experience of being murderers we would still be a long way from the experience of being *murdered*. (If in those days we had had the slightest flicker of belief in life beyond the grave, I know we would have killed ourselves.)

Lunatics. So much time had to pass before we realized that we could sell those pistols for good money and then pay the rent for the attic with it.

Once again, Billy Wiseass, you scold me for my egoism. You write: "It would be better if you wrote a novel in the style of *Daphnis and Chloe* or something like that," in order to "liberate yourself from the first arson." (Here apparently you slipped up and typed—I

23

hope it wasn't intentional—"from the first arson" instead of "from the first person." So, what were you actually thinking: to liberate myself from the first-person form or from the first flame? Don't forget to clear that up for me.)

Eh, bien! Let's just say I am heeding your sage advice and I will satisfy your curiosity. So send me the exact number of rats, mice, and cockroaches that were in the attic on the day (which day was it?) of our meeting. I only remember that you found some pretext to leave the room. And be sure to send me the prototype of the woman I'm supposed to describe "in the style of *Daphnis and Chloe*," as you put it.

But don't forget: if Chloe is Eurydice, then I must be Orpheus!

Oh, and I haven't made any progress at all on the lute.

Think it all over carefully!

P.S. Your presence in this poem about love bothers me, but I can't avoid mentioning you here and there. Of course I will be considerate and will refrain from describing you. (Haven't I already betrayed you that way once?) It is more than enough that I have to keep cropping up as "I" from page to page, as if I were some imaginative concoction or confabulator.[1] Or a phantom.

---

1. This word is derived from the word *fabula*; Billy Wiseass uses it in this sense. (Author's note.)

THE JOURNEY, OR THE CONVERSATION

The Bay of Dolphins (No date)

My dearest, my one and only. A light-year always passes between two of our embraces. You know how distrustful I am of love letters, and yet I must write to you. How can I give evidence of my love if you cannot see my eyes or behold my nights?

I would rather write to you about this place, about the people in the Bay of Dolphins. This region is odd, my dearest. If I weren't bound to my attic by an unusual, sick passion, I would settle here. But of course, only if you wanted that too, only if you liked it here too. Here we could revel in lunar honey . . . But who can think about that right now?

Today I went on a dolphin hunt with the natives. We boarded a little schooner they called *Haramakana* or *Karamahana* or something like that, and we waited for the moon to shine. Then we rowed, silently, reverentially, on the liquid gold, our boat festooned with wreaths of wild magnolia, so that we looked like a funeral procession or a wedding party. I don't want to make you jealous and I won't be describing their women. Although you have no reason to worry. They interpret my skin color as a sign of pallor and anemia, so they're as sympathetic toward me as if I were a sick man.

They were all infinitely sad and formal, and I didn't know what was really going on with them. When they very adroitly threw a dolphin into the boat, they cried, mutely, like we do in Europe for the dearly departed. There was no wild ritualistic dance of the type we might imagine taking place. There was dignified sniffling, sincere and proud, unimposing and quiet.

"You don't need to lie," said one native to me when I brought a handkerchief up to my mouth in a gesture of courtesy.

"I just want to blow my nose," I responded.

"Then that's another matter," said Tam-Tam. "You white people lie a lot. You think it's beautiful and decent to want to share someone else's pains and joys, by hook or by crook. For us that is a sign of rudeness and bad upbringing. What reason, for example, could you have to cry right now?"

"Because of the dead dolphins . . . Just like you, I might add," I said, blowing my nose with the handkerchief to show that I was being considerate and not hypocritical.

"What ideas you have!" said Tam-Tam. "Crying on account of the dolphins! We are crying because we have to slap the moonlight with our oars."

Their oars were barely touching the water.

I do not know, my dearest, if I will ever be able to mail you these letters, but I'm writing them to you nonetheless. There's no sort of postal system here, and nobody has heard of that civilized European aberration called "the letter" or "correspondence." But I am writing to you because I consider the monologue to be a highly dishonest and selfish thing. I would kill myself the moment I realized that I was sufficient unto myself and that I could be satisfied with a monologue. But, if I succeed in mailing you these letters somehow, it means I'll be depriving myself of the pleasure of letting you discover in my eyes the moonlight from the Bay of Dolphins.

Do you know how these savages profess their love?

When a boy is mature enough for tender intimacies—that is, when he has tried his hand at all the vices and gotten burnt out on orgies—he goes, on the day of the Pan-Dolphinian celebrations (a day that falls on the first of May, which is the seventh of January according to our calendar—when the moonlight is thickest and at its most resonant), to the girl who has come to him in his dreams more than seven times. Doing this, however, is considered—perhaps with justification—a great disgrace, or even a mortal sin, for a grown man. For us Europeans these are incomprehensible and amazing things. We would simply conceal the fact that we had dreamed of the same beloved seven times, or we would inform the parents of the girl that we were ready to wed their one and only (insofar, of course, as our material circumstances vouchsafed us the right to make such a proposal). In their society, though, telling anyone that a man has dreamed seven or more times of a woman is considered a mortal sin and a desecration of the sanctity of sleep (what I mean is that they believe that to use their meager language, which consists of only 300,000–400,000 words and an equal number of symbols, to make a fabulous description of the images and content of dreams amounts to an absurd and pretentious act of blasphemy); on the other hand, not admitting such a significant and fundamental fact is considered hypocrisy and an example of "Europeanness"; and then there's the fact that they consider a man who is incapable of dreaming seven times of the same woman to be a simpleton and an idiot, and so they poke his eyes out to make sure he cannot see the moonlight on which they are dependent and to which they are connected by bonds of blood, as we in Europe are to the sun and to hypocrisy.

So this is how things work in the Bay. On the day when the moonshine is most resonant, the young man takes his chosen one by the hand and leads her up onto the *Tanga Sihaka* (Rock of Love). There, in the moonlight, he looks deeply into her eyes without speaking, for hours upon hours. Then, after this mute confession, after this mono-dialogue, he takes a sharp *tahinj* (a kind of curved dagger) from his waist and slices open the blood vessels on his left arm. The whole time he never takes his eyes off of her, so that she can follow the life being extinguished in his pupils, and his eyes turning white. Then, when she feels that she loves him too, she takes the knife and . . .

"And if she doesn't love him?" I asked of Tam-Tam.

"She'll become enamored of him while he bleeds," he said.

"But still . . ."

"Then she allows him to die at her side. As soon as the sun goes down, she rips out his heart and tosses it to the dolphins. That's why dolphins have a weakness for love."

"Remarkable," I commented. "Why is it done this way?"

Tam-Tam continued with a pedagogical air: "Because, after a night in which a man admits that his heart is not his own, his heart isn't good for anything at all. If the woman to whom it was sacrificed will not take it, then it's only fit to be thrown to the dolphins."

"Cruel stuff," I said, almost to myself, but he appeared to have understood me because he stated afterward: "We brook no compromises like you Europeans. I think that this is all honorable: who would be so insolent as to offer up the same heart a second time?"

"Wise Tam-Tam," I said. "And what happens with those folks on the crag who have sliced open their arteries?"

"Nothing. They love each other."

"I know," I said. "They cut open their own arteries."

"Holy Moonlight, are you ever naïve!"

"What do you mean, naïve?" I asked. "Did you or did you not say that they cut open their own veins?"

"Maybe I told you that, but who knows if they really do it . . ."

Today, after the Pan-Dolphinian ceremonies and orgies, I asked Tam-Tam to help me translate the song that they sang yesterday evening to the accompaniment of tom-toms: the song that received the most votes in the competition at the choral festival. But before I get to that, I want to tell you how the selection and voting were carried out. After each number was announced, a singer came out to an improvised podium and sang his song. Then, when he had finished, the people present tore out hairs from their heads, as many as they wanted. These hairs were collected in a dish made of seashells and at the end they were counted by specially trained parrots that cried out the name of the winner. Tam-Tam had ripped out a whole handful of hair on account of this particular song, so this morning I could see a bald spot the size of an egg above his forehead.

At first he agreed to the translation, but then he grew concerned. "It's difficult," he said.

"But still, Tam-Tam, let's give it a try."

After some convincing, Tam-Tam started singing, sitting right on the shore of the bay, in the shade of the palm trees:

> *I brought her shells and pearls from Senegal*
> *(My liver is bleeding from all the diving)*
> *I brought her coral from Kokovok*
> *(I broke my fingers while digging)*
> *I tore the teeth from the mouth of a shark*
> *(This grappling left me covered in scars)*
> *And I braided all of it into her hair*
>
> *Once I didn't turn up for ages after a hunt*
> *(Leviathan dragged my boat far out to sea*
> *and it's a shame about the harpoon)*
> *and like a woman I returned, overwhelmed,*
> *with nobody there to welcome me on the beach*
>
> *But in the hut I found my dearest,*
> *Who had shorn half her hair*
> *And combed out the pearls and coral.*
> *And I thought: she's mourning for me*

But in the hut I found Ngao-Ngaa,
Picked the lice from her hair like Thaki the ape,
Gathered pearls and coral like a parrot,
And then I wanted to eat Ngao-Ngaa
But that would not make her hair grow

Afterward I set out over the sea
that I might seek my Leviathan,
that I might tear my harpoon from his back
and drive it into my own heart,
because my beloved had shorn her hair
and scattered her diadem of pearls
and coral

All of this because of Ngao-Ngaa

That afternoon I showed him my polished translation of the song.
   He shook his head:
   "You did not hear this song from me."
   "But I did, Tam-Tam," I said. "You sang it for me this morning
in the palm grove."
   "No," he replied. "I sang you the song about jealousy that starts with:

Aagn oagn gobz evs—

and you got it all distorted. We call that *ailongam.*"
   "What does that mean?" I asked.
   "*Ailongam,*" he said.

"Translate it for me."

"It cannot be translated."

"What do you mean it can't?"

"That's one of the twelve thousand words in my language that one cannot translate. Ninety percent of the words in your song are also untranslatable."

"Impossible," I said.

"Then translate it yourself!" he said, in a tone that was almost uncivil.

"Magnolia!" I said.

He just grinned, as if he wanted to let me know that he was no longer angry.

Or perhaps it was because the orange-colored moon had come into view and poured out its resonant silver over the entire Grove of Magnolias where we were strolling, lost in thought.

You will say to me, Billy Wiseass (to hell with you!), that there is too little here concerning the things I really want to talk about.

It might seem that way to you, Mr. Know-it-all!

But she is ubiquitous, like the moonlight in the Grove of Magnolias, like my writing, my breathing, and the sonorous "oh" that she utters from time to time in the pages of this book. That sound is the presence of her shadow. It is her sigh, and it accompanies me.

Or is it perhaps my own sigh, O all-knowing one?

You will be wondering, Capricorn, who the hell I'm looking for in this exotic land of adventure and turmoil.

I am certain you're wondering about this—provided that you haven't changed.

You are well aware, my dear old friend, that I cannot live without our good old attic, without my lute, without Eurydice.

There you have it: I fled from myself and am now putting my love to the test.

But I know that I am going to return a light-year older (I didn't say "wiser"), and I know that I will once more put my arms around my lute and my love, Eurydice.

Igor, I wanted to describe Eurydice, to compose a poem worthy of her name. You were the first to tell me, Capricorn, that I should drop the joking and stop chasing rainbows.

Do you remember that conversation of ours in the attic?

I said: "Fine. I will take your advice. I'll move down to the ground floor and write a novel about Marija the Prostitute. About her lovers and her abortions."

You: "All right. Do that. I'll be sorry to see you leave our attic, but do it—for the sake of the poem!"

Me: "It's not a poem. It's not going to become a poem."

You: "A poem about a whore named Mary Magdalene."

Me: "No. A story about the abortions of a certain Marija, known as 'the chaste.' A novel about the socio-historical, material, (a)moral, ethnic, and ethical causes of her ruin. A novel about Marija's aspirations. A novel of the city."

You: "You're making fun of me."

Me: "God forbid!"

You: "You know very well that I wasn't thinking of a fable but rather of ambiance. Are you with me? An atmosphere nourished on debauchery and hope. That's what I was thinking of."

Me: "But how do you envisage this *atmosphere nourished on debauchery and hope*? Won't that turn out to be a fable? But I want to write a book, Igor, a book! Without Marija's maxipads and without her lovers, without dialectics and ethics. Even without Eurydice."

And in conclusion, Capricorn, haven't I told you a hundred times that I am writing in order to emancipate myself from my egoism?

RETURN

In late autumn I returned to the attic. I climbed the stairs excitedly, lugging my heavy backpack loaded with shells and the seeds of exotic plants. I had brought a gift for everyone: for Eurydice a necklace of dolphin teeth and a conch named Mandragora, for Igor a shrunken head from Equatorial Africa, and for the old cleaning lady a seven-colored reed mat.

"This is for you, Madame Witch," I said. "It can be used as a doormat."

"Where did you swipe this from?" she asked darkly.

She looked closely at the iridescent rainbow in the folds of the mat.

"I got it from an aborigine. His name was Tam-Tam. In return, I had sex with his wife."

"You ought to be ashamed of yourself," she said.

"Alas," I replied, shrugging my shoulders.

"But where is the Billy Goat?" I asked. "Surely he hasn't yet learned to walk quietly in the corridor and wipe his feet at the door?"

"I'm sorry, who?" she asked, blinking.

"Igor," I said. "From the attic. Billy Wiseass."

"Oh, him. You know, he moved down to the second floor. He's working now. He says he's writing a novel. 'So why are all these women coming to see you?' I ask him. 'Those are my models,' he says."

"Well, how do you like that!" I said. "*I'm going to have him thrown out.*"

"Watch your step or I'll have you thrown out, dearie!" the cleaning lady snapped.

"I just meant," I said in appeasement, "that I would have to ban him from *my place* up there. What the hell am I supposed to do with that confabulator?"

"Don't call him that! He has talent."

"How do you know?" I said.

The blush of a teenage girl spread across her pockmarked face.

"Well, you know, I'm also, um, like . . . a model," she said, almost in a whisper.

"A model?!"

"Yes," she said. "In that thing that Mr. Igor is writing, I will be a—a cleaning lady."

"But you are one already!"

"Yes, but Mr. Igor says that in his novel I will be the *prototype* of all cleaning ladies. Me as myself, plus all the rest."

"*And how does Mr. Igor plan on accomplishing that?*" I asked, out of both curiosity and envy. "How does he intend to make a 'prototype' out of you, when you're already what you are? Surely you're not going to pose nude for him?"

She thought about this for a while, then she just shrugged her shoulders:

"I trust Mr. Igor," she said. "He's so sweet and so talented."

The first thing that took me by surprise when I opened the door to my good old attic was the odor of dankness and urine. Igor's black trousers swayed on their hook, and I flinched. It's not easy to see one's good friend hanging. Even if it is only symbolic.

Otherwise—at first glance—nothing had changed.

Yet the cranes had flown from the walls. And there wasn't a trace at all of the wild doves; the mastodons and reptiles lorded over the place by themselves. Their teeth had grown alarmingly long.

"Well, now!" Igor said unexpectedly behind my back. "As you can see, old boy, nothing has changed."

We embraced.

"Where is that stench coming from?" I inquired.

"From the rat poison," he said. "Vermin and rats are rotting in the cracks."

"How clever!" I said. "The things you keep coming up with!"

"There's that derision again," he said.

"I brought you something," I said, to avoid a fight. "Hang on just a second."

I proceeded to dump the shells into the middle of the room, and moonlight spilled out of them like crystals.

"What the hell is that supposed to be?"

"What the hell is what the hell supposed to mean?"

"But those are just ordinary shells!"

Then I picked up the loveliest conch, the one with the richest sound, which was about the size of a chamberpot, and tilted it up against his ear. "Listen," I said. "Do you hear anything?"

Gradually his eyes filled with tears and shame. And possibly with remorse, too.

You birdbrain, I would've killed you if you'd remained consistent. But now what can I do? It's utterly inconsistent of *me*, but I'll tolerate your affable presence and your help.

I prized the shell away from his ear. "Here's a handkerchief," I said. "Wipe your snot. This is hypocrisy and Europeanness. You've grown a touch sentimental."

"That's because of the novel," he said with a sniffle.

"What kind of novel?" I asked, feigning astonishment. "You don't mean you've given up astronomy?"

He started stroking the conch shell disconcertedly.

"No," he said. "You know, old man, it's like this . . . I've fallen in love."

"Bravo," I said. "That's a good thing. It's no reason to cry."

"Her voice is like the moonlight from the Bay of the Dolphins."

I winced. How did he know anything about my orgies in the Bay of the Dolphins? Then I saw the luggage tag from Tam-Tam's native land on my backpack.

I let out a laugh.

"That's the last thing I need," I said. "For you to fall in love too. Then who will stay sober and track the phases of the moon, and the constellations? It'll be pure hell."

I was too tired and agitated to go out searching for Eurydice that same evening. By the way, our European custom of only receiving visitors until 8:00 P.M. is most irksome. It doesn't even take into account whether the moon is full or in its last quarter.

I hung up my trousers on the peg next to Igor's and dutifully brushed the sand out of my tattered tropical coat; then I shook out the stardust. Afterward I washed my feet and lay down to dream. I was fed up with prose.

"Knight errant!" she said.

"Eurydice! Eurydice!"

The rains of autumn started up again.

I carried her in my arms across dark streets. I held her high above the muck.

"You are still the same, sweetheart," she said.

We were approaching the railroad embankment, toward which something was always drawing us. Memories. And piles of faded leaves in the ditch.

I placed her on a bed of foliage and began to recall her embraces. Her eyes. Her scents.

"Your hands have grown harder, sweetheart."

"From the oars," I said. "From the winds."

No, I didn't say anything. I inhaled her breasts, went blind.

The next day I cleaned up the attic a bit and reached once more for my lute. I spent the entire morning tuning its strings. It had fallen ill during my absence, grown deaf. It must have perceived my fingers on its slender neck as caresses.

Otherwise, why would it have lamented?

It took several hours of great patience for me to find its former resonance and tone. All at once—that is, completely by itself—it remembered its voice; from out of its dark insides poured a flood of pearls, as if from a colossal shell.

Then it seemed to me that someone was knocking, and I stopped playing for a moment.

"Would you knock it off already?" said the cleaning lady, rapping on the plywood door with her key.

"I'm done," I said. "Excuse me."

"As far as I'm concerned, you can strum on that thing as much as you like. But the tenants are complaining that they can't enjoy their siestas after lunch because of your flute."

"It's a lute," I said.

"Well, fine," she said to appease me. "A flute."

I drank bitter woodland tea and ate half a pack of zwieback with butter. Then I stretched out in the rocking chair to rest, since I couldn't play. There I sat, with my eyes closed, for about half an hour, and then I stared at Venus's thighs on the ceiling. Above one stately knee the dampness had drawn a dark blot that resembled a large wart. I shifted to my side and lit a cigarette.

That's when Igor arrived.

"Sorry to wake you," he said.

"Have a seat," I said. "I was just napping a bit."

"Okay," he said, sitting down on the bed. "I need to ask something of you."

"Say . . . You haven't gotten into a jam with her, have you?"

"How did you know? Did the cleaning lady tell you?"

I burst out laughing.

"I just had this presentiment," I said. "You fell out of the stars and right onto her!"

"You're in a joking mood," Igor responded. "But this is a very pressing matter."

"How many months along is she?" I asked.

"Two."

"What do you intend to do now, Billy?"

He shrugged his shoulders and turned his eyes upward. That was how God looked when he surveyed the world on that seventh and final day of Creation.

"I don't know," he said. "That's why I came to you."

"Write a novel," I said.

"Can I have a cigarette?" he said. "I'm nervous."

"But of course."

"I have to confess something to you," he said, after we had lit up. "Only, please don't misunderstand me."

"I'm listening."

"I started it," he said. "The novel."

"Well? Go on."

"That's not the issue," he said. "The problem is that I don't know how it is going to end. I don't know how all these things are going to unfold . . . And I've got no money for the abortion."

All at once I grasped the seriousness of the situation.

The girl can die, I thought. Or she can give birth to a baby girl. Or she has the option of aborting.

My God—so many possibilities!
But she definitely has to have the abortion.
This is as urgent as it gets. Otherwise—*voilà, a new character*!

I am very much afraid, Billy, you dimwit, know-it-all, sonofabitch, Igor, devil—*I am very much afraid that you might become a hero.*

What will become of you if you don't scrape together the money? You'll get all kinds of notions that you *are* a hero, a martyr, a Don Juan, a man of sorrows, cavalier, victim of your passions, he-man, sensualist, seducer, daredevil, father, husband, citizen, debtor, spouse; you will become socially aggrieved, politically reactionary, sectarian, conspiratorial, humiliated and marginalized, insurgent, ostracized, oppressed; you will be a good-for-nothing, a gelding, an accursed poet, a defender of the poor and needy, patron, man of compassion—to sum it up in a single word, you will be something like a *character* in a novel, a *hero*, or even—a *category*.

Believe me, I would never utter your name again.

Alas! If only I could contribute something toward this abortion of yours with my old lute!

But for that kind of money you couldn't even get the lowliest midwife from the other side of the tracks to soil her hands.

It rains so often here that the moonlight is splashing.

Eurydice, put your arms around me!

You aren't always the same, either, you who appear in the likeness of Eurydice, from out of the words, shadow, and veil. On the outskirts of the city your voice spreads luxuriantly, peacefully across the windows, like dusk, blue. In the moonlight it starts to resonate—like a harp, like . . .

But in the attic, toward evening, when your breasts are bare, your voice becomes a caress, a miracle, a violet blossom.

"My beloved, you're kind of quiet today," she said. "How can you be sad when I love you?"

We were standing under the bridge, watching as the cloudy green water whirled off into the twilight.

"I don't know," I said. "Why do people always flip off the lights when the caresses begin? There's only the occasional flicker of a candle or glimmer of twilight."

"Oh," she agreed. "You're right. Tenderness is . . ."

"Why did you stop? Say it: tenderness is . . . ?"

"I don't know, it's . . ."

"This dreary rain is to blame for everything," I said. "And this gloomy water. Let's get away from here. To the movies. Or to a café."

"It's late," she said. "I'm also feeling a bit melancholy. I can't put my finger on it . . ."

"It isn't late. I've got an idea. Let's go to the attic. Why didn't we think of this before?"

And there we were, climbing up the slick steps, holding hands as lovers have done since time out of mind. Upstairs the glow from the streetlights overcame the gloom. The rain fluttered like a swarm of tiny insects around the chandelier. Our pale shadows quivered in the puddles on the shimmering asphalt.

"You're wearing a new dress," I said, as an excuse for gazing at her. And then I heard her answer.

"New? You are conversant with my wardobe?"

"I am right, am I not?"

"Yes. I recently had it made here. Do you like it?"

"Very much," I said, letting my gaze pass over her again before casting my eyes down. "Do you want to dance?" I added.

"Would you like to?" she asked, her brows raised in surprise, but still with a smile.

"I'd do it, if that's what you want."

"You're not quite as well-mannered as I thought you were," she said. When I dismissed this with a laugh, she added: "Your cousin has already gone."

"Yes, he is my cousin," I confirmed quite unnecessarily. "I also noticed a while ago that he had left. I'm sure he's taking his rest cure."

"*Nous causons de votre cousin. Mais c'est vrai*, you are all a little bourgeois. *Vous aimez l'ordre mieux que la liberté, toute l'Europe le sait.*"

"*Aimer . . . Aimer . . . Qu'est-ce que c'est! Ça manque de définition, ce mot-là.* What one man has, the other loves, *comme nous disons proverbialement*," I contended. "I have been giving freedom some thought of late," I continued. "That is, I heard the word mentioned so often, that I started thinking about it. *Je te le dirai en français* what I've been thinking. *Ce que toute l'Europe nomme la liberté est peut-être une chose assez pédante et assez bourgeoise en comparaison de notre besoin d'ordre—c'est ça!*"

"*Tiens! C'est amusant. C'est ton cousin à qui tu penses en disant des choses étranges comme ça?*"

"No, *c'est vraiment une bonne âme*, his is a simple temperament, not prone to dangers, *tu sais. Mais il n'est pas bourgeois, il est militaire.*"

"Not prone to dangers?" she repeated with great effort . . . "*Tu veux dire: une nature tout à fait fermée, sûre d'elle-meme? Mait il est sérieusement malade, ton pauvre cousin.*"

"Who told you that?"

"We all know about one another here."

"Did Director Behrens tell you that?"

"*Peut-être en me faisant voir ses tableaux.*"

"*C'est-à-dire: en faisant ton portrait?*"

"*Pourquoi pas. Tu l'as trouvé réussi, mon portrait?*"

"*Mais oui, extrêmement. Behrens a très exactement rendu ta peau, oh vraiment fidèlement. J'aimerais beaucoup être portraitiste, moi aussi, pour avoir l'occasion d'étudier ta peau comme lui.*"

Then I gazed mutely a while longer at the ceiling, at Venus's thighs. How selfishly had I grown accustomed to this new role! My God! What an amorphous stain these thighs of Venus were in comparison to this skin!

"Let's do that," I said mechanically again. And so we went on speaking softly, our conversation covered by the piano. "Let's sit here and watch, as if in a dream. It is like a dream for me, you know, for me to be sitting here like this—*comme un rêve singulièrement profond, car il faut dormir très profondément pour rêver comme cela . . . Je veux dire: C'est un rêve bien connu, rêve de tout temps, long, éternel, oui, être assis près de toi comme à présent, voila l'éternité.*"

"*Poète!*" she said. "*Bourgeois, humaniste et poète . . .*"

"*Je crains que nous ne soyons pas du tout et nullement comme il faut!*" I responded. "*Sans aucun égard. Nous sommes peut-etre* life's orphans, *tout simplement.*"

"Joli mot. Dis-moi donc . . . Il n'aurait pas été fort difficile de rêver ce rêve-là plus tôt. C'est un peu tard que monsieur se résout à addresser la parole à son humble servante."

"Comment? C'était une phrase tout à fait indifférente, ce que j'ai dit là. Moi, tu le remarques bien, je ne parle guère le français. Pourtant, avec toi je préfère cette langue á la mienne, car pour moi, parler français, c'est parler sans parler, en quelque manière—sans responsabilité, ou comme nous parlons en rêve. Tu comprends?"

"A peu près."

"Ça suffit . . . Parler," I continued, *"pauvre affaire! Dans l'éternité, tu sais, on fait comme en dessinant un petit cochon: on penche la tête en arrière et on ferme les yeux."*

"Pas mal, ça! Tu es chez toi dans l'eternité, sans aucun doute, tu la connais à fond. Il faut avouer que tu es un petit rêveur assez curieux."

"Et puis," I said, *"si je t'avais parlé plut tôt, il m'aurait fallu te dire vous!"*

"Eh bien, est-ce que tu as l'intention de me tutoyer pour toujours?"

"Mais oui. Je t'ai tutoyé de tout temps et je te tutoyerai éternellement."

"C'est un peu fort, par example. En tout cas tu n'auras pas trop longtemps l'occasion de me dire tu. Je vais partir."

It took a while before what she had said penetrated my conciousness. But then I started up, looking about in befuddlement, like someone rudely awakened from sleep. Our conversation had proceeded rather slowly, because my French was clumsy and I spoke haltingly as I tried to express myself. The piano, which had been briefly silent, struck up again . . .

"What are you going to do?" I asked, flabbergasted.

"I am leaving," she repeated, smiling in apparent amazement at the frozen look on my face.

"It's not possible," I said. "You're joking."

"Most certainly not. I am perfectly serious. I am leaving."

"When?"

"Why, tomorrow. *Après dîner.*"

Something collapsed inside me. I asked:

"Where?"

"Very far away."

"To Daghestan?"

"*Tu n'est pas mal instruit. Peut-être, pour le moment...*"

"*Soit... Laisse-moi rêver de nouveau après m'avoir réveillé si cruellement par cette cloche d'alarme de ton départ. Sept mois sous tes yeux... Et à présent, où en réalité j'ai fait ta connaissance, tu me parles de départ!*"

"*Je te répète que nous aurions pu causer plus tôt.*"

"So you would have liked that?"

"*Moi? Tu ne m'échapperas pas, mon petit. Il s'agit de tes intérets à toi. Est-ce que tu étais trop timide pour t'approcher d'une femme à qui tu parles en rêve maintenant, ou est-ce qu'il y avait quelqu'un qui t'en a empêché?*

"*Je te l'ai dit! Je ne voulais pas te dire vous.*" Then, wearily, I extinguished the candle. The book fell with a bang onto the straw. A solemn stillness enveloped my thoughts, my sleep.

Adieu, mon prince Carnaval!

Igor, I created Eurydice. I sang her form into existence!

I was able to follow from day to day the metamorphosis of her breasts, growing round under my hands until they became as fragile and delicate as the finest Chinese porcelain.

I made her hips dance, made them bloom, made her waist unfold like a lily.

I seasoned her tongue with chamomile and hyacinth; I sharpened it with kisses, unbridled it.

Igor, my friend, I transformed her fingers into endearments, into caresses, into a lute.

Her arms I ennobled, transformed into a bolster for my head, into a dream.

I turned her into my own selfishness, my friend Igor, into a sigh, into breath.

And what is left for me to do now, Capricorn, other than pull my own hair out, or poke out my eyes?

Brother Igor, she wrested away my selfishness, my masterpiece!

THE LUTE, OR THE GRAND FESTIVAL

"Get up!" said Igor.

I didn't open my eyes. I just listened to him plucking the straw and ripping the paper from the window. Then two or three small pieces of glass hit the floor through the fine straw, and a draft of air struck me.

"Get up!" Igor repeated. "You cannot take refuge in sleep. I brought you a little beef broth and a shot of cognac. That'll bring you back to life."

"Close the window, Igor. Please. You can see that I'm shivering all over, that my teeth are chattering. And I can't even open my eyes in this burst of light."

"Will you eat then?" he asked.

"Let me have a sip of the cognac. My tongue is rotting."

He brought over his little flask and poured a few drops into the lid.

"Don't act preachy," I snapped. "Just hand me the flask."

"Okay, okay," he said. "Kill yourself with it for all I care. You haven't eaten anything for days and you won't come to your senses. You're going to go nuts like this."

"So what if I go nuts? At least I won't be conscious of anything."

"Just a little soup," Igor said, guiding the spoon to my mouth. "And enough of these dark thoughts . . . So, what really happened?"

"Nothing happened," I said. "Everything is perfectly fine."

"Eurydice . . ."

"Shut up!"

"Well, well, look at that," he said. "You've gotten as mean as a junkyard dog. But I'm simply asking as your friend: What's going on with you two? Something's obviously not right."

"Everything is fine. (Sorry, but I'm really irritated.) Why shouldn't it be? She loves me, I love her, and . . . so there."

"Nonetheless," he said. "Something happened during your absence. Surely she didn't . . ."

"You are a vulgarian, Igor. She's not that Marija from the ground floor . . ."

"Still, something happened. That's clear enough. Ultimately, even your Eurydice is no angel. Even she . . ."

"Igor! If you say anything obscene, I swear I'll kill you. I don't know with what, but I'll kill you."

"All right!" said Igor. "This means that your old egoism is back. You're cured. You've recovered."

"Give me a cigarette," I said, "so I can thaw out."

We smoked for ten minutes without a word. The soup gave off steam and, together with the aroma of the tobacco smoke, the vapor gave the attic a new odor.

I only drank one more little glass of cognac.

Afterward I spent several months in the attic, neither receiving visitors nor going out. I grew a beard like a hermit. Serpents hatched under my nails.

I had ripped the lute's hair out so it wouldn't provoke me. I plugged up its mouth with dirty rags so that it couldn't sigh and couldn't hear.

Day and night I reclined in the rocking chair, staring at the ceiling. I listened to the gurgling of the rain, the grieving of the winds.

From time to time Igor brought me unsweetened tea with toast and cigarettes. I was choking on my own stench, in the smoke. I had forgotten how to see and how to speak.

I was a coward for not killing myself then. Or wise.

Freshly shaven, and in my sumptuous black tie, I was seated before a succulent leg of chicken in a café. I had a white napkin across my knees and the sleeves of my coat were rolled up so they wouldn't get worn out. I was no longer drinking either dark, flavorsome wine or scorching absinthe. I had only mineral water and a soft drink. Voraciously, with my nose in the foam, I gulped down a beer.

"I barely recognized you," said Billy Wiseass.

I offered him my hand in greeting without getting up.

"Well . . . filtered cigarettes, uh-huh, and *real* mineral water, and . . ."

"Cut it out!" I said. "This is not some roadside dive."

I saw the malice in his eyes. He was getting ready to say something unpleasant to me. Maybe to remind me of the attic. To rub my nose in it and stain my sleeves. I waited, nibbling away at the drumstick. A bone had gotten caught in my throat.

"You're not even going to offer me a seat," he said. "Look, even if you're angry at the whole world, that's still no reason. . . ."

"Sit down," I said.

I saw that he had something to tell me.

"Do you want a beer? Waiter!"

"A cognac," he said. "A double shot, please."

"How's your Urania?" I asked. "I haven't seen you two for a long while."

"Fine, thanks," he said. "Oh, yeah—I almost forgot. Perhaps this will interest you . . ."

"Out with it already!" I said. "You're cooking up something malicious, aren't you, you dirty rat."

"Eurydice!" he said.

I plunged my nose into my plate.

He repeated: "Eurydice. I said 'Eurydice.'"

"So what?"

He grabbed me by the arm. "She's waiting for you in the attic, you moron."

"Very nice," I said. "But first I have to pick this bone clean. I'm not going to leave this chicken to the cooks out of sheer charity!"

"I haven't seen you for ages," the cleaning lady said when I came running up.

"I've been sick," I said.

I expected her to ask me for the rent.

"Sick? And I didn't even know. Otherwise I would've paid you a visit. So what was wrong with you?"

"Influenza," I said.

"And just what is that?"

"Bloody diarrhea," I said and then rushed up the stairs.

I had already raced up two floors when I heard her voice: "A girl was waiting for you."

"Are you talking to me?" I asked, panting as I leaned over the wobbly wooden banister.

"To you . . . Who else? She left less than five minutes ago. If you hadn't been licking your plate, you would've caught her."

There was still a warm indentation on the bed where she had been sitting. The window was wide open and the wind reverberated in the lute. She had taken the rags and paper out of it. The ashtrays were gleaming, and the books, which previously had been lying strewn about in the corners everywhere you looked, had been piled up into a burial mound.

Orpheus, a note read, *why do you claim the right to suffer for yourself alone . . . ? I waited for you until 9:30. I could tell by your lute what kind of shape you're in. Can't you even . . .*

I couldn't read the rest.

So there we have it, Igor. A few light-years older, but so young, and so bitter.

And what would have become of us if we had kept on acting and pretending?

You know very well, Capricorn, that I wouldn't have lasted very long rolling up my sleeves and drinking mineral water and smoking filtered cigarettes.

53

What would we be like without journeys, without conversations?
How would I fare without my lute, without Eurydice?

"You have to look at things realistically, dear fellow, *realistically*," said the man whom we are here calling Billy Wiseass or some such thing.

"I agree with you completely," I said. "But don't forget, my good man, that it is especially necessary for people like us: artists. And even for you, the astronomers, too. Through the twinkling of the stars you're supposed to glean hints of the aroma of the astral humus, the social composition and political structure of the galaxies. After all . . ."

"You're wrong," he said. "The point is not to intuit an object, as you say, but rather to investigate it, *tangibly*, to touch it and feel it. Without any sort of guesswork, my dear fellow."

"What do you mean?" I asked. "I assume you can't feel the stars with your hand as you would the udder of a cow."

"Why is it that you always want to be witty, at all costs? I'm tempted to say: a professional wit."

"Out of egoism," I said. "That is to say—by mistake. In actuality, fate has allotted to you the role of *reasoner* and wiseass (your name states as much), just as I have been given the lute as my lot . . ."

"I've had it up to here with that lute of yours. A stupid, pompous, antiquarian symbol."

"*It is not a symbol at all!*" I said.

"What the hell is it, then, if not a symbol?"

"A *lute*," I said.

He waved his hand dismissively: take a hike.

We walked on in silence for some time. We were still such good friends that the silence didn't bother us. The hollow clatter of our footsteps hardly made us flush with embarrassment.

"Take a look at this, Igor," I said, pointing at a large yellow poster.

Or was it he who pointed at the big yellow poster and said: "Take a look at this, Lute-meister . . ."?

At any rate, the poster was there, yellow, damp with fresh glue and rain, looking like some enormous rose petal. On it was written, in beautiful black letters:

GRAND FESTIVAL OF
FASHION
Autumn-Winter
with a Revue of Coiffures,
Flowers,
and Pop Tunes

"Let's go, Capricorn," I said.

Or he said: "Off we go, guitar-meister."

At any rate, we headed in that direction . . .

At the door they asked to see our passes. Igor pulled out a thousand-dinar note and slipped it into the man's hand. The guy took a look at us and then gave us two pornographic postcards; the program was printed on the back of them, along with the words "No Admittance Under Sixteen Years of Age."

"No matter," I said. "I would make a point of attending out of professional curiosity, even if I were under sixteen . . ."

Billy the Goat laughed. "That's a good way to put it," he said.

"*Flowers grow on the dung-heap*," I said sagely.

"What do you mean by that? What kind of flowers?"

"Nothing, nothing. I was just thinking out loud. Besides . . ."

"Why do you always stumble to a stop before you finish your thought?" he said. "What kind of flowers are at issue here?"

"The ones that are sprouting from me. With their roots in my heart and their blossoms in the sunlight. With their pollen in my eye . . . Those are the ones."

?!

After some sort of incident—I don't remember what—Eurydice either couldn't or didn't want to come see me in the attic anymore. Maybe it was after that note she'd left me while I'd been licking my plate clean in some pub. I don't know. I no longer even know if that attic ever existed or if I just conjured it up. And I also don't know if Eurydice ever climbed up into that attic through that narrow, dirty stairwell, where the cockroaches rustle about when the light catches them by surprise. Then, with a light crack, they squish under your feet like berries. A little greasy spot remains; it spreads out and becomes darker the farther it gets from the epicenter of the eruption. I don't know—I don't believe—that she ever climbed those filthy steps. But then where did that slip of paper come from, which I found at some point under the bell jar next to the rocking chair? Maybe she passed the note to the cleaning lady downstairs in the hall, and then she put it under the bell jar so the rats wouldn't shred it like lettuce. Who knows if I ever really read this note? Or whether she, Eurydice, really wrote it with her own hand. But I can't believe that I planted this note here myself. For God's sake, how would I have been able to imitate her handwriting so skillfully . . . ? It truly was odd handwriting. And worthy of further comment. At first glance it resembled Sanskrit. To tell the truth, I've never actually seen Sanskrit, but in any case I think that Eurydice's handwriting has its roots in some secret dream. In places her writing was utterly illegible. All the consonants looked like a single letter, which looked like all of them together, so that you could never determine precisely which was intended. Each and every vowel was also written identically, with the one difference that you could at least produce its sound: that eternal letter—a multitude of circular, oval, large-eyed and bewitched letters rolled around between those indeterminate, exotic consonants. Come to think of it, everything she wrote looked like it contained only one and the same imperishable letter, so that her words, once written, scrolled past like a vague tolling of bells. But I never had sufficient time then to ponder all this. I was always completely preoccupied with deciphering her notes, which I found unexpectedly here and there, most frequently right in the attic upon returning from my travels. These really weren't missives in the true sense of the word. On a slip of paper ripped from a memo pad she would string together a necklace of sighs, with pretty much every other little square containing either an O, or a kiss, or a tear, or an eye. *It all depends on who's reading them, and how.* And of course on what the word denotes outside of its pictorial meaning. Such a letter-kiss, a letter-poem, had ten, or a hundred, variants and interpretations, and I believe that my fate was sealed by one such misunderstanding. I would remind you of that well known, historic misunderstanding which resulted in the godhead being represented with horns instead of a halo; thus Moses became a garden-variety cuckold, ridiculed in secret by everyone in the neighborhood—beginning, of course, with the cleaning lady. And the fact that one venerates him in public, or even prays to him—that is, I believe, the result of hypocrisy. But one should not forget to observe a moment of pathetic reverence: even a cuckolded godhead does inspire respect, after all.

"You've really gotten carried away, Cuckold," said Igor, peering over my shoulder. "I'd bet my life that you no longer know what you're talking about."

"I do know," I said, offended. "About the horns! And next time don't stick your nose into my papers."

"What horns are you talking about?" he said. "About yours? That's obviously the reason you started hiding your papers from me."

"About your horns," I said, in the calmest possible voice.

He grew a bit more serious, and then exploded in laughter. "Maybe you're just a big jerk, banjo-meister. A joker is what you are."

"I was talking about horns," I said again. "About yours . . . and about mine. I wouldn't joke about such things. You know that quite well."

He stopped laughing. All at once he grew as pale as . . . well, simply pale, like . . .

"It's not that . . ."

"Uh-huh," I said, nodding my head. "Forgive me for having to tell you this . . . You know . . . this is unpleasant for me, but since you already . . ."

"Just go on," he said quietly, clenching his teeth. "I can take it."

"Marija . . ."

"I know. She was making out with someone in the lobby of the building."

"No."

"Something more serious? She didn't . . .?"

"No," I said impatiently, "but it's simply that . . ."

"Maybe it's simple for you!" he cried out and slammed the binoculars to the ground.

"That's a shame," I said. "And to think that tonight they'll be celebrating the 'golden wedding anniversary' in the constellation of Orion."

"I don't care," he said, with his head thrust into the palms of his hands. "Finish telling me what this is all about or I will kill you."

"Take a look at this," I said, handing him the postcard that I'd gotten at the Grand Festival of Coiffures, Flowers, and Pop Tunes. "I have no choice but to show you this . . . It wouldn't be fair."

He grabbed the Marija-postcard out of my hand and held it closer to the light.

"So what?" he said. "That's Marija. What are you trying to say? This particular number is called 'Unforgettable Pussy.' She strips to the tune of the Persian March for a whole fifteen minutes . . ."

"And you knew about this?"

"Of course," he said. "I got her this gig . . . Is that all you had to tell me about Marija? Just that?"

"Isn't that enough for you, you old goat? Isn't that enough?!"

He doubled over with laughter, blushing, and his tears flowed down like . . . His tears were gushing out because of the laughter. When he had calmed down a bit, he pulled out his wallet, which

59

was made of donkey leather and adorned with initials of mother-of-pearl, and he silently handed me another postcard. Then he went back to rolling around in the straw, convulsing with laughter.

Oh, Capricorn . . . why didn't you spare me this?

Why did you help me destroy that monument of gold, flesh, and moonlight?

Oh, Eurydice: the image, the shadow—the whoring viper!

WALPURGIS NIGHT, OR THE BEGINNING OF FORGETTING

I recall that it was at the outset of the long, painful Walpurgis Night.

"I can hardly wait to get horizontal," said Dirty Pussy, squeezing my arm.

I said nothing. It was the beginning of Walpurgis Night.

"Do you live far away, Tomcat?"

"Uh-huh," I said absentmindedly.

"And your folks aren't at home?"

"No," I said. "They live several stories above me. Way up on the top floor."

Then I fell silent. We walked a while, without talking, across the bumpy cobblestone streets of the late-night suburb. Her mouth reeked of *kakaform* and her hair stank of shedding cat. From time to time, she rammed her tongue in my ear, so that I practically had to run along in front of her.

"Why don't you want to flip on the light?" she asked, as she entered the attic.

"It's an idiosyncrasy of mine," I said.

"Then at least put me in the bed," she said.

I began to undress her without turning on the light. I only left her her silver-and-black slip, which was the color . . . the color of snakeskin. (I recognized the colors more by their scent than by their feel under my fingers.) She stuck her panties into a red plastic tote bag. I heard the zipper whirring as she opened and closed it. Then I took her in my arms and whirled wildly several times around the room. When I had distracted her in this way, I placed her on the straw that was lying on the floor. She got up in a hurry.

"You tricked me," she said. "You don't even have a bed in your room, Mister!"

"I sold it," I said. "But don't get formal with me. As you can see, I'm plenty informal with you."

"I was raised that way," said Dirty Pussy.

"But still," I said placatingly. "You shove your tongue in my ear and then you call me 'Mister.' That's not right. One must be completely naked. Without a condom on the tongue."

"You're just a run-of-the-mill poet, nothing more," she said. "And you'll always remain a poet. And nothing more."

I recoiled, insulted.

"How do you know that? It wasn't . . ."

"You're just blabbering away. That's how."

"Aha," I said, now relieved. "I thought maybe I had called you something like Eurydice . . . or . . ."

"Did you sell your bed on account of her?"

62

"No," I answered. "I was kidding. I'm having it chromed. I'll be ready tomorrow. I think it will be ready . . . tomorrow."

"Eurydice or the bed?" she asked mockingly.

I clenched my teeth. (Had I dared utter that name in front of her?)

"The bed! . . . And don't ever say that name again!"

"*Eurydice, Eurydice, Eurydice—how's that? Eurydice!*"

"Please, don't! I implore you!"

"Eurydice!"

At that moment I swung my fist in the direction of her voice. I felt her teeth sink into my hand. Then I covered her mouth tightly with the palm of my hand so that she wouldn't be able to spit her teeth out. I was afraid that the neighbors, or the cleaning lady, would hear us. It had already been two months since I'd paid any rent. She twisted out of my grasp and scraped me with her grubby fingernails. This riled me up, and I started squeezing her harder and harder. A moment later I felt her arms descend gently around my neck. That was when I removed my hand from her mouth. Then I pressed my lips to hers. Just in case.

"You're good at that," she said, spitting out one of her eyeteeth.

"Oh," I said, feeling flattered. "I'm actually not quite myself tonight."

"You're gentle, Mister," she said. "I don't like brutes."

"What did I say about being formal with me?"

"I was brought up to do that," she said, and I heard her unzip her little tote bag. "Put on my underwear for me," she said with a whimper. "The straw is poking me."

Obediently I raised her leg. Corpses are dressed with the same attentiveness after they are washed.

Then I lit a cigarette. I smoked for a while in silence. A clear beam of moonlight glided through the attic. Like the distant tones of an accordion. Then it disappeared, unexpectedly.

I was thinking of Eurydice.

Around four in the morning we set out from the attic. A cold, raw wind was blowing, showering us with needle-like snowflakes. I wrote down her address and accompanied her to the first streetcar of the day.

When I returned, I still had the taste of her skin in my mouth. The taste of rancid meat and goat's blood.

The next day I sold my lute at the flea market. After that I went to the post office and wired half the money to Dirty Pussy's address (77 Walpurgis Vista Road). With the rest of the money I bought a large bouquet of white carnations and took them to her in person. I wanted to apologize to her for being vulgar and inconsiderate.

She met me in a colorful nightgown made of Chinese silk. She had done up her hair like a geisha. And on her feet I noticed pearl-studded Arabian slippers.

"Well, what do you know!" she said when she caught sight of the flowers. "Didn't I say that you were some kind of poet? Flowers and women . . ." And with that she took the bouquet out of my hands. Then she chucked it into the garbage can standing by the door. Before the carnations landed, I saw maxi-pads blooming luxuriously amid the trash. Fortunately the flowers then blocked the sight of them.

"Don't you like them?"

"They're beautiful," she said. "But my doctor prohibits me from having them. I'm allergic to flowers. I always break out in a rash . . ."

"Sorry," I said. "I didn't know. If I had . . ."

"It doesn't matter. It's okay," she said.

"How are your teeth?" I asked, in order to break the silence.

"Fine," she said. "I put in my spare dentures. The other ones were worn out anyway."

As soon as I had paid that visit, I felt terribly hungry, but I couldn't eat. My hands disgusted me, as did my mouth. That's why I went and bought a small bottle of alcohol and a bar of pink soap. I bathed and scrubbed myself with a sponge all morning long, until they threw me out of the bathhouse.

"What's wrong with you?" asked the woman at the counter, when I handed her the money for my visit to the *hammam*.

"Nothing," I said. "I'm just a little scorched."

My hands and face, and indeed my whole body, were one giant scald and blister, in which the lymph wobbled at my every motion. The strong alcohol solution I had rinsed with chewed up my mouth.

For several days I was unable to eat anything. As soon as my temperature had fallen a bit and I could move again, I popped into Pygmalion's and ordered myself a bottle of gin.

"Shall I wrap that up?" the waiter inquired.

"No," I replied. "Just bring me a big glass."

Then I drained the whole glass at one gulp. Afterward, dear Igor, I vomited, vomited so beautifully, so passionately.

Igor, my brother—my eyes were clear, my hands were innocent like those of a maiden. My hands, comrade Igor—

"*See to it that you get them dirty,*" came Igor's response.

"What?" I said. "How's that?"

"Well, you know," he said. "How long do we intend to remain sleepwalkers?"

"I don't know, Igor. I regret what happened to my hands."

"Cleanliness has infected you the way syphilis does," he said. "It's messed up your head. I still maintain that the only medicine is prostitution and lust. Physical therapy."

"I know, Igor, I know. But I'd prefer to kick the bucket this way. And, by the way, I've already tried it all."

"You have not," he said. "You have not."

"For instance?"

"Yellow Fever!"

"Give it to me immediately!" I said. "Infect me!"

Igor called the waiter over and ordered two pomegranate juices, two cognacs, two maraschinos, two glasses of palm wine, two gins, two shots of whiskey, and some other drink the name of which I forget. Then he shook it all up and stirred it with the little silver spoon he always carried with him. Next he put in a little mint, rhubarb, vanilla, and clove, and then squeezed in several drops of essence of violet.

"Down the hatch!" said Igor.

"Down the hatch!" I whimpered. "To the spirit of Eurydice!"

The taste of vanilla reminded me of her mouth.

"It's already been a light year since you sang anything," Igor remarked. The fever had dulled his eyes.

"Not since I sold the lute."

"So start up again," said Igor. "Say: 'I don't give a shit about the lute.' Say it."

"I don't give a shit about the lute."

"Thaaaaat's it . . . And now sing something," he said, twirling the little silver spoon inside the empty glass.

I launched into a song, bellowing:

> *A rose petal will be your pillow,*
> *and tulips will mourn your footsteps . . .*

"Lute-meister, Lute-meister!" exclaimed Igor. "The same old song again."

"Sorry, Billy. Forgive me."

Then Billy Wiseass chimed in with his silvery voice:

> *Your pillow will be a petal that rests on thorns,*
> *And Lute-meister will forever grieve over you . . .*

Then I intoned:

> *Tulips will blossom in your footprints,*
> *And you will fall into the arms of a blockhead!*

"Bravo! Bravo, Lute-meister," Billy screeched, clapping his hands hysterically. "Now that's what they call 'therapy.' Long live yellow fever! Long live the blockheads! Down with sleepwalkers!"

At dawn we regained consciousness under a table, in a condition beyond excruciating. Between the two of us some naked, grungy body was sleeping the innocent sleep of a child, hands stretched out above her head. Her eyes were half open, dark violet. Her breasts sagged down onto the filthy, spit-covered floor, their tips poking into the dust. Slowly it all dawned on me. I remembered that Igor and I had wrenched her away from some sailor types in a quayside bar. The ache on the top of my head and Igor's black eye reminded me of that much. At first it was a fistfight, until a red-headed sailor raked a beer bottle across my head. But Igor and I managed to reach the bar. At first she was rooting for the sailors, but when we got hold of the bottles and started toppling the drunken seamen, she began laughing so hard she bent double and started cheering for us. In the end she gave the victors a big wet kiss on the mouth and ordered herself a Yellow Fever. On our tab.

"To the conquerors!" she said and raised her glass.

"Whore!" snarled Igor, fingering his eye.

Then I broke in: "The only medicine is prostitution and . . ."

"Whore!" Billy repeated. He hurled his glass to the ground.

She was bent double with laughter.

"She's a bitch," said an offended Igor. "At the beginning she was rooting for the sailors . . ."

"But later she was for us," I said. "Right?"

"She's a sneaky bitch," Igor repeated as he started crying. "They're all alike. Even whores are dishonest. Even whores!"

"You haven't tried everything yet, comrade Igor," I said, moved by the emotion of it all.

"Everything. I've tried it all," he said. "Whores were my last hope."

"You haven't tried Red Fever yet," I said. "Isn't that right?"

Igor regained his composure. "Do you know the recipe? For real?"

"Waiter, waiter!" I panted.

"What can I do for you?" said a new character as he executed a bow.

"Mix us a cocktail with everything imaginable . . . And put a dash of vanilla in it. And some window-box sage . . . And don't forget the shot of primrose bitters either, and, to top it off, a spot of delirium from poppies and henbane."

"And three glasses," interjected Igor.

He held up three fingers in front of his eyes, as if in amazement. Then he repeated: "Three."

In those days I was hideously bored in the attic. Maybe I missed my lute. That silly, idealistic clamshell. To pass the time, I started practicing jujitsu. Then I acquired boxing gloves and a punching bag.

"You've gone crazy," said Igor.

"I'm amusing myself," I replied.

"Why don't you read something?" he suggested.

"Nonsense," I said. "You should've just read those sailors some poetry that night at Pygmalion's to try to get that Mary Magdalene away from them."

"Don't tell me you mean to imply that I didn't kick enough ass that night?"

"No, you fool. That's exactly the point. You kicked ass all right and . . . you earned Mary Magdalene."

"So that's why you're practicing your boxing? To win Eurydice?"

"*She does not exist*," I said, irritated, and launched a series of punches at the bag.

"Who are you hitting?" Bill Goat asked maliciously.

"I'm beating the Lute-meister on the head. I'm knocking some sense into him," I said, gasping and pounding myself in the mug till the blood flowed.

Then I began learning Sanskrit and Polynesian dialects, but I soon realized that there was no point to this, so I switched to English. Soon I was giving private lessons to the sluts of the port. Never before had I had pupils who were more diligent and compliant. And they paid me regularly. In kind, to be sure. How else? Then I stopped giving lessons to those girls who lived by the Bridge of Sighs, as we referred to them. Every day their madam had brought me coffee with a great deal of sugar and milk, just because once I'd said that I liked it. She was convinced that I was a good boy, even a good pedagogue; she did say, though, that I should smoke less and not study so much. She especially recommended that I not smoke before breakfast, on an empty stomach.

"That is the only thing in the world, ma'am, that's worthwhile," I said. "Smoking."

"There's some great disappointment in your past . . ."

"No, no," I said. "But I prefer a bitter cigarette to sweet coffee with sugar. It's simply . . ."

Then she said suddenly: "Listen, it's not nice of you to make your café latte sound even sweeter than it is, *just so I'd end up coming across as all the more insipid*. You reporters are all the same. It goes without saying that I'm mentioning this in your interest. And in the interest of my girls. It could have unpleasant consequences for them . . ."

"Don't worry about anything, ma'am," I said in comforting tones. "There are people who really like a lot of sugar in their coffee."

"Nonetheless," she remarked, "don't mention my girls' names in that thing you're knocking together. And move the plot over to another part of the city. Say, for instance, 'by the Bridge.'"

"But why, when you don't live by the bridge but rather by—"

"But I implore you—"

"Oh, forgive me," I said. "Next time I'll be more considerate."

CHEZ TWO DESPERADOS

Igor suggested these names: "Salvation Harbor," "Last Chance," "Dos Desperados," "Chez Orphée," "The Broken Lute," "The Two Pistols," and a few others that we rejected out of hand as too banal: "The Shore," "At the Sign of the Three Palms," "A Summer Night's Dream," "The Bay of the Dolphins."

"I'm sorry," I said, "for not contributing anything to all of that. Nonetheless, Igor, you will admit that I myself could have thought it all up as easily as you. You just happened to be the first to start listing them. Just say so: that's the way it is."

"You're welcome to consider yourself the first one to say them," Igor countered. "By the way . . ."

"I know. You want to say that I'm making all this up anyway. But, you see, I won't admit that to you. Well, maybe just the pistols. They were my idea. But one could just as easily assert that you anticipated them yourself."

This conversation took place at the end of summer, on the coast, as the sun was going down. We watched as the waves pitched the sodden seaweed onto the beach, giving the smooth-faced quartz a red beard. We were seated in front of a small *taverna* on which we had just put down a deposit. We were supposed to start renovating at the end of autumn, as soon as the previous owner had moved out. He was an old man who was hard of hearing and sold only beer and absinthe, and nobody frequented the place except for longshoremen, worn-out, pockmarked sailors, and various old salts. The old guy griped to us that he'd had to fire a sixteen-year-old girl he'd hired because the sailors had slapped their hands against her rear end so much that her buttocks were soon bruised the color of a sailor's undershirt.

"Would you agree to stay on as *maître d'hôtel*?" I asked the old man. "You'd earn more than in the past. And, who knows, maybe later on . . ."

"Nope, nope," the old man said with a sardonic smile. He had watery, suppurating eyes and he sprayed saliva as he spoke.

I wiped my face with a handkerchief and asked him once more if he would stay with us as a waiter, or headwaiter, if that suited him better. In view of the fact that he spoke Italian and various dialects, he could act as our interpreter.

"No," he said sadly. "Everybody patted and groped her, everybody except for me. And some of them were even older than I. That's why I fired her. I couldn't stand to watch the way they all fondled her."

At that point, Billy got right in his face: "Will you stay with us? Stay here! With us!"

"Nobody prevented me. But I couldn't. I simply couldn't do it," the old guy said. "And they were all slapping her. 'Leontina, a spritzer!' and then a deafening smack on her buttocks."

"It's super that you were actually able to hear that!" said Igor with irritation in his voice. "So is that how you went deaf?"

"For sure!" said the old man, glumly. "I couldn't keep watching that. That's why, one evening three or four days ago, I said: 'Leontina, in case you . . .'"

"Let's leave him alone," said Igor. "It doesn't seem like he's spoken with anybody about this till now, and he wants to serenade us strangers with it like an old frog . . . Nevertheless, we will have to look for this Leontina."

Our idea for a little taverna was truly outstanding. Since we were disappointed with everything, and as incapable of love and unqualified for life as we were, we resolved to withdraw from the world. But because we weren't able to take off to some deserted island, as we had intended at first, we decided to open a restaurant and bar in a small town along the coast. Both Igor and I like the autumnal peace and quiet in these isolated little towns with their narrow streets. Therefore we had resolved to sell all our stuff and save all the money that we earned from giving private lessons to the girls and whores of the city, and then we would rent a little taverna and dedicate ourselves to our studies.

"This is the only way that one can study life," said Billy Wiseass. "*Books are an invention. Stories for toddlers. But we will gather around us all kinds of desperados* (we especially liked this word in those days) and listen to *authentic* stories, *authentic* life experiences. Only that will constitute the true school of life," Billy explained excitedly.

I joined the game with enthusiasm:

"It is not we who will have to go out into the world; the world will come to us. Bringing the best that it has to offer. Ships will provide us with sailors, in whose eyes we will discover continents and climates, landscapes and horizons . . . Everything, Igor, everything! We will only accept those people who have seen as much of life as a living person can! Only the ones bearing scars . . ."

"The ones with callouses . . ."

"The ones from the streets . . ."

"The ones from distant lands . . ."

"The ones who lowered their colors . . ."

"The ones with no future . . ."

"The ones with colorful pasts . . ."

"The ones without love . . ."

"The ones who have already experienced everything . . ."

"Seen everything . . ."

"And desire nothing more . . ."

"Nothing . . ."

"Don't you think," I said, "that it would be good for us to accept women as well? Raunchy harbor chicks? The kind who carry profound mourning in their eyes."

"Provided, of course, that they have remained chaste. Without hackneyed tales of infidelity, betrayal, misery, rape . . ."

"The ones who have sought love . . ."

"And not found it . . ."

"The ones who have loved, body and soul . . ."

"Body and . . ."

"And with their whole Body and . . ."

And they wandered through the world so wide
embracing everything they did find.

Then Igor picked up where I left off, or vice versa:

And now they pursue their requiems
for their white bodies

"For their white bodies."

The specialty drink at the Two Desperados restaurant—a specialty that Billy Wiseass especially envied me for inventing—had the very prosaic (and, incidentally, blasé) name "The Desperados' Pistol." On our menu, it was located right after the Wiener schnitzel *and it cost the same.*

I couldn't blame Igor if he was jealous; it was really a devilish idea!

We got an order for it right away, on our first night of business.

The customer had a red, puffy face with bags under his eyes. He stared at the menu for a long time with his beady, watery eyes. The menu was bound in golden-green snakeskin and the letters on the cover were emeralds:

CARTE DE VINS OF THE
TWO DESPERADOS TAVERNA

IMPORTED WINES
Malaga à la Orpheus
Eyes of Eurydice
Desperados' Dream
Magnolia Maraschino
Glutteus aeburnea à la Leontina
Satyr's Ambrosia
Gelosia vecchia al Umberto
Brandy à la Mansarde
Arpeggio à la Mansarde
Žilavka Mistress of the Lute
Hosszú lépés Smart Ass
Thea-Lipovanka á la Mary Magdalene
Evening Star, bitter
Morning Star, violet
The Song of Tam-Tam
Moonlight of Delphi
Palm Frond Vugava
Primavera marina
Mezzogiorno adriatico
Cyclamen Sailor's Duel
Le temps retrouvé
Dollente, lis blanc
Allegro, ma non troppo
Allegretto (108), red
Allegro vivace (152), white
Ritardando brillante, maestoso
Doloroso espressivo

Dolce, ma con fuoco a l'Euridice
Desperados' Soliloquy
Boule-de-neige
Il Sueño della Vida
Balata, bitter opal
Tourmaline bicolore
Tourmaline rose (rubellite)
Saphir cagochon
Calitera menandar (Asia)
Precis heleida (Madagascar)
Precis eurodoce
Anea Orphilochus (Sumatra)
Arhonias Bellona (pierides)
Byblia ilithya
Agerona mexicana
Chrisidia madagascariensis
Eucalitia clemante
Amethyst blue (sapphire)

DOMESTIC WINES
Fruška Gora Pearls of Dawn
Dubrovnik Madrigal
Ohrid Legend
Gračanica Dawn
Slavic Legend, bitter
Morning Star over Herzegovina, bitter
The Highways of Prince Marko (dark)
Scutari Gold (gutedel)

Mother Jevrosima's Hair
Banović Strahinja's Goblet
Lazar's Bicep
Vuk Mandušić's Dream, white
Maternal Curse
Word of Love
Simonida's Eyes
A Monk's Manuscript

And then, as far as the food on the menu went—

FISH AND SEAFOOD
Dragonfly in mayonnaise
Poison d'avril
Barbus de Sumatra in palm oil
Danio Rerio with lemon
Egg of Columbus
Girardinus Guppi (Arc-en-Ciel)
Chinese warrior with mint
Barbillon Galapagos
Aquamarino adriatico
Speckled lutist with mustard
Flying coral with French fries
Seaweed with spaghetti
Mistral with orange
Mistral in olive oil
Mistral from the grill
Mistral in a tin can

South African diamond
Gavial of Celebes
Tahitian pictor
White Tahiti-flower with rice
Rouge-Gorge of the Adriatic
Rouge-Bleu of the Adriatic (with cream)
Tomatoes with Greek olives
Tern with eggs
Bouquet de mariée with mustard
Cleaning lady in lemon juice
Shark à la Sumatra
Ageronio Atlantis
Catenofele salicia (Nymphalisis)
Hvar Guitar without Sordino
Hvar Guitar with Sordino
Brač shipwreck in white wine
Rose of the winds

As he pored over the menu, a cut diamond in the shape of a skull and crossbones twinkled on his short index finger. I observed the way his fingers slid perplexedly over the snakeskin.

But, finally—after he had drunk an absinthe—the man said, "The specialty of the house, please."

His voice wasn't trembling when he said it.

"How's that?" blinked the old man Barba-Umberto, whose eyes were following Leontina's butt under her black apron as she walked away.

The man with the swollen eyes cast a brief glance at Leontina, who was washing glasses behind the bar. Then he repeated:

"The specialty of the house. A Desperados' Pistol . . . That's what it's called, isn't it?"

Barba-Umberto blanched.

"They promised me that they would look out for her. I said: 'Boys, if anybody so much as taps her a single time on the . . .'"

Then Igor jumped in:

"What may I bring you, sir?"

"A Pi-stol. A Desperados' Pistol. How many times do I have to repeat myself?"

"Excuse us," said Igor, wiping the crumbs off of the Brač marble in front of the man with a white napkin.

"Our interpreter is a bit hard of hearing . . ."

"A double. Don't forget: a double."

"As you wish." Billy bowed formally and headed to the bar, as the man called out after him:

"*Noch ein Bier!*"

Igor bowed.

The man had hooked his short little thumbs into his suspenders and was watching the dark, wintry sea through the window. A black and white ship was trying to draw up to the breakwater through the waves. From time to time its howl could be heard over the wind and it immediately awakened in me the memory of a train embankment, of Eurydice.

Next to me I sensed the haste with which Igor was working. He unfastened the pistol from its hook (where it hung over the bar like a museum piece), and then I heard him cock it and eject the four remaining bullets from the magazine. After he had inserted one bullet into the barrel, he brought out a silver dish from under the bar. He wiped it off and then laid a small white silk napkin, folded into a triangle, onto it. Carefully he placed the pistol onto the napkin. He was then ready to head to the table but something else occurred to him. I noticed that he was agitated, although his hands weren't trembling. He moved the napkin with the pistol over to the side of the tray, and on the opposite side he placed a mug of foaming beer. Then he nodded to Barba-Umberto and handed him the tray, motioning with his head toward the guest with the skull-and-crossbones. The man was still watching the ship roll around right outside the entrance to the harbor. Without a word Umberto took the tray and set it in front of the customer. The man with the suspenders glanced at the pistol, poked around at it intently with his small index finger, and then drank down his beer. Then he sat there for another quarter of an hour, immersed in the sight of the ship. Then he gestured to Umberto to bring the check.

"This is too hard," he said in German. "An excellent imitation. *Eine schöne Imitation*. But very hard. I don't want to bust my teeth. *Auf Wiedersehen!*"

Umberto brought back the tray with the empty mug and the pistol. He was muttering something to himself, of which I was only able to catch the words: *porca miseria, porca miseria*.

The stranger had not left a single dinar as a tip. *Porca miseria!*

No. That's not how it was.

First he drained the mug. Then he wiped his mouth with the back of his hand and lit a cigarette. When the cigarette had burned down to his fingernails, the man stubbed it out in the ashtray. There was desperation and determination in this gesture. He licked the barrel of the pistol, and I saw Barba-Umberto making idiotic faces at him. Then a shot rang out. It was so unexpected that even I started.

He did not fall over backward, as I had expected. Rather he slumped forward with his face on the marble table, as if he were dozing.

Umberto covered the blooming skull with a white cloth. Billy was screaming hysterically into the telephone receiver: "Hello? Hello? Hello?"

"It had to be this way," I said in a conciliatory tone, almost to myself. Then I hung the pistol up again on its hook above the bar. Naturally I had already reloaded the magazine.

Barba-Umberto held up unexpectedly well at the interrogation. Billy was kind of nervous. We were fined a trivial sum.

But the memory of the Island never left me, even for a moment. This time I said nothing at all to Billy Wiseass about it. *I wanted to liberate myself from my selfishness.* That's why I told him nothing. Right up to the day I left, unexpectedly. My God, it was also quite unexpected for me.

To be honest, the idea of a taverna was nonetheless an excellent one. Not only because we would then no longer need to knock about in filthy harborside dives (if Muhammad won't go to the mountain . . .), but also because it allowed the world to come to us (. . . then the mountain will come to Muhammad). Everything that we had ever imagined became reality. We were not to be trifled with!

We wanted to purchase—that is to say, we did purchase—every kind of musical instrument possible, from accordions to Tahitian guitars. Otherwise we provided no music. The guests were informed by means of the menu that the instruments were at the disposal of anyone who knew how, and, of course, had the desire to, play them. Thus, late one winter evening, we had the chance to hear a young woman (I never saw her again) play Debussy's "Clair de lune" on her harp. Her dignified features betrayed her affinity with the nostalgic and anachronistic sense of refinement of the nineteenth century. She had sickly, dark green eyes and pale, fragile hands. While she played, her hair fell onto the gilded baroque harpstand and concealed her face. Never before had a Corinthian column been crowned with a more noble capital. Her long fingers, with nails the color of old silver, glided over the strings, and everything would have ended beautifully if Barba-Umberto hadn't wanted to stroke her hair. Her fingers paused on the strings as if they had been bewitched. She then swiftly put the harp aside and took her blue raincoat from the hanger. She didn't even turn around as she exited. She made use of the general astonishment and disappeared forever.

"You, Barba-Umberto, are a regular moron," I said, when we had pulled ourselves together. "A mo-ron!"

"So you think so too?" he said, like an idiot.

"Moron," I repeated. "A senile moron."

"Indeed, I've never heard anybody play more beautifully either," came his naïve reply.

Igor practically jumped down his throat and said testily, "He's telling you that you're an idiot. Nothing but an idiot! *Capito*?"

"You are right, my boy," said Barba-Umberto. "Indeed, I never even saw hair like that in Constantinople . . ."

"What do you think?" Igor asked, turning toward me. "Is he pretending to be crazier than he really is . . . ?"

"What else could it be?" Umberto interrupted. "*It seemed to me that moonlight was dripping through her fingers.*"

I swear to you that this feeble-minded old Umberto said exactly that: "I had the impression that moonlight was dripping through her fingers."

Can you imagine? That idiot, Umberto!

We wanted to become wealthy, powerful. In order to buy ourselves a yacht (it had already been named *Eurydice*, what else?) and sail the seven seas, visit all the continents. Of course our first mission would have been to visit the Bay of Dolphins. *To verify its existence.*

So who says that it isn't out there somewhere?

"Look, this is why we must resort to *poison and dagger*," said Igor. Or I was the one who said: "To poison and dagger."

"Salted sardines aren't poison."

"At any rate," we said, "they make you hellishly thirsty. Therefore everyone should have a barrel with sardines close at hand. Free poison."

Thus we bought a barrel of salted sardines and put it in the middle of the taverna, at everyone's disposal. We assigned Umberto and Leontina the task of placing a few sardines onto the little ceramic plate in front of every guest, so that everyone would drink at least a liter of table wine afterward. We were counting on human greed.

That's how it all began. And, sure enough, everything went well at first. Late on winter evenings we listened to sailors' laments on the accordion; we became the port's confessional; we became the resonant seashell that sings with the voice of the Sirens when you hold it up to your ear. Here and there burned a candle or two, and at "Desperados" people were always singing as piously as they would at Mass.

But soon everything went to hell in a handbasket, in the way that only a dream can go belly up. We became a hangout for bums, a nest of thieves, a bordello, a snack bar where generous portions of salted sardines are handed out for free. We became a gambling joint, a forge for foul, pithy curses, a den of bloody showdowns, a font of outrageous vices and pathologies.

I swear: all of this could really have happened. It was all so beautifully conceived!

Igor, my friend, we have nothing left except the desert island! Did we not give our word ages ago that we would never kill ourselves? *For the sake of a moment in the future!*

Do you remember our conversation? In the attic—where else?

You: "Why don't you kill yourself, Lute-meister? I know you're just a shadow of your former self without Eurydice."

I: "Mephistopheles! Satan!"

You: "Kill yourself. Be done with your shadow. You were not born to compromise."

I: "And I didn't compromise."

You: "So isn't Eurydice just a shadow as well? Tell me, Lute-meister: what is she?"

I: "The Ideal, Satan. The Ideal! The life-principle, if you will. That's why I will not kill myself."

You: "A striptease-ideal! Was it not *you* who asserted that the ideal 'was not allowed to have freckles'? Did you not say, Lute-meister, that God could not become an ideal for you because He makes compromises with evil? Were you not gloating over the fact that you wouldn't even bow to the sun, since it has spots? Did you not, my little lutie-pie, cease worshiping your erstwhile Eurydice (is that what she was called?) *as soon as you got close enough to her to see the freckles on her nose?* Did you not assert that the ideal, Eurydice, is not ideal if it isn't perfect?"

"Silence, Billy! I'll kill you, Satan!"

"Kill your own self. Out of consistency, at least . . . Or make a compromise. Reconcile yourself to the fact that the sun has spots. And bow to it!"

"Igor, you devil, why are you tormenting me? Why are you leading me into temptation?"

"I'm just pounding some sense into you. If you can't resign yourself to the fact that the Eurydice-ideal—"

"Then I should kill myself . . . ! Is that what you mean to say?"

"Yes. What will become of us if we aren't capable of understanding an ideal *metaphorically*?"

"What do you mean 'metaphorically'?"

"That's easy: conditionally. The sun—"

"We should deal with freckles. Sunspots. That's what you want to say."

"Bravo, Lute-meister. Precisely. As pure as the sun. When you draw close to her, when you cast a shadow over her: freckles. That's Eurydice, the ideal. Can you accept that, ideal Lute-meister?"

"I don't know, Igor. I just don't know. Didn't I tell you that even the sun—?"

"And you? And you . . . ? So are *you* without freckles? Aren't you—?"

"You fool! This isn't about me. I'm the least important person on the planet. Maybe that's precisely the one good thing about me. That I am searching for the ideal, Eurydice. As my opposite. Do you get it? *As my opposite* . . . That's why it's hard for me, Igor. But I shall not kill myself. But *I can kill myself* when I want to. *That's* what you don't want to understand."

"So what are you going to do? You can't live like this."

"I'm heading off to the Island . . . Do you remember that island I always used to tell you about in moments of eclipse, moments of crisis?"

"And?"

"And, and, and . . . ? That's where I'll think everything through. To kill myself or—"

"—to compromise with the ideal, with Eurydice."

"—or not to kill myself . . . Right. That's the same thing as compromise."

THE ISLAND, OR THE JOURNAL

I've struck a deal with a farmer to tend his cows on the island for the winter. This island is called Isle. Every Saturday (save when it's very stormy), the farmer will bring me enough food for a whole week.

Water is my only problem. I have to get used to unsalted food. I am gradually getting accustomed to it. *Cum grano salis.*

I live in a stone hut about five hundred yards inland. (This is the same hut I slept in five or six summers ago when I vacationed here.)

February 22

These cows are not much trouble. From time to time I unleash Argus so that he can drive them southward. To the west there is a gigantic gorge, with lush greenery along its rim, but the earth around it crumbles and slides in easily. I was told to be careful there, because two years ago a milch cow plunged down the cliff.

February 23

The island is much bigger than I had thought. At first this discovery depressed me. But now I am playing Robinson Crusoe.

And laughing.

February 24

Robinson regrets not having brought along a handbook of medicinal herbs. The callouses from the big oars—with which the cows are ferried over, one by one—remind him of the existence of another world.

Robinson pounds his forehead. He shakes out the powder from the folds of his tobacco pouch onto his blisters.

February 25

I am lying on the low, hard bed, covered with a sheepskin coat. The flames from the fireplace illuminate the eyes of my half-German shepherd napping at my feet. Outside a storm is raging. I hear the wind driving the waves against the rock face.

February 28

I have not caught anything to eat. I roamed to the south, but I did not discover any tracks in the sand.

I will have to set out fishhooks.

Beginning of March

I waited in ambush with my rifle cocked and ready. Actually this was only a game—I would never shoot birds. Much less an eagle. I was just looking through the sights. It flew out from a sheer cliff and started soaring in a great arc. At first I could still see a snake clamped in its claws. Then the eagle changed into a black dot.

Into a star.

Today I made it down to the southernmost point of the island.

After having passed through the thick underbrush, I emerged onto a rugged, bare patch of sharp, fissured karst.

In the pitted surface I discovered deposits of sea salt. I have a hard time believing that the waves reached all the way to these heights!

I surmounted the crest with the ease of someone who had spent his entire life on rocky terrain. But I did bruise the bottom of my foot a bit when I leapt from a bluff down onto the sand of the beach. Then I continued my march southward on a little tongue of land running along the base of the cliff. At first Argus ran in front of me, but later he was dragging himself along in the footprints of his master, his tongue hanging out like a mangy bitch's.

In the company of the first star of the evening I reached the southern extremity of the island. I gazed at the star, prepared to christen it "Narcissus," when it suddenly faded out.

A lighthouse! A lighthouse!

I lay exhausted on the beach and wept. Argus was whining and wheezing over me. Then he started to bark. From above, from the lighthouse, he was answered by the hoarse barking of a small dog.

On our way back the sumptuous moonlight lit up my path.

When I am familiar with the entire island, every stone, every leaf—what will become of me then?

One cannot live from the past.
Nor from the present . . .
— — — — — — — —.
— — — — — — — —.
I shall leap from the hillside . . . There, where the earth crumbles and slides!

ATTIC (II)

Osip told me this morning that the most beautiful thing in the world is to give gifts with no thought of gain for oneself.

But I've started at the end. Here's the way it was. (Immediately following my return.)

I met Osip in the crowd of people outside the cinema. He was waiting for Marija. I knew he was waiting for Marija because he was impatiently looking over his shoulder and smoking nervously.

"Marija doesn't want to wear the fur coat," he said as soon as we had shaken hands. "Can you imagine?"

"What fur coat? I've never seen her with a fur."

"Didn't I tell you? I bought her a fur for her birthday."

"Oh, boy . . . Where did you get that kind of money?"

He just smirked and then pulled me aside.

"Do you want to give Eurydice a fur coat for her birthday, too?"

"Don't you know?" I asked. "I'm not with Eurydice anymore . . .

But, how is it that you're giving away furs like they're going out of style?"

"Why should I tell you, when you have no one to give one to? That's a shame. They make beautiful gifts."

Then he went ahead and told me how he does it. (I think I'm the only person on earth in whom Osip really confides. He believes that we're very similar, except that I haven't yet revealed my true nature to him.)

And this is how he does it. He goes into a department store at a time when the crowds are at their biggest (usually right before holidays) and asks to see the fur coat that he likes the best. At least this is how he bought the coat for Marija. The salesman fills out his invoice and sets about packing up the coat. That's when Osip inquires, with pronounced politeness, "And where is the cashier, please?" "Over there. Straight ahead and then left." Then Osip, apparently distracted and surprised, says: "Oh, right. Thanks very much." He heads for the cash register. After that, unnoticed by anyone, he pulls from his pocket a small stamp bearing the inscription PAID. He tears off the part that stays with the cashier, returns to the counter, hands over the receipt, takes the fur, bows politely, and . . .

"I would perish from fright," I remarked.

"It's quite simple," said Osip, flattered.

"What do you mean, simple! If it is, then why don't you buy yourself a suit that way, instead of freezing to death in that topcoat and rags?"

"Look, here's the deal. There's a difference. Your way would be pure theft and nothing else. Do you understand? Pure theft. My hands would tremble, or I would get sick and throw up . . ."

"And your way?"

"Well, my way achieves a certain balance of power, if I may say so. One party is robbed, while another party is gratified. The only important thing is that the accounts balance. That an equilibrium is established. You see, the salesperson won't be punished, because it will be determined that my stamp, although a dead ringer for theirs (I make them with just as much minute detail as a delicate, tiny engraving) is actually only handmade, and consequently counterfeit . . . And Marija gets the fur coat. She'll feel that she is adored, that she is esteemed . . ."

"And how do you profit from all this? If I may use the word 'profit'?"

"Of course you may," replied Osip. "I am the last creature on earth who would do something without benefit to himself . . . I get a great deal out of this. Above all: smugness. I think it's obvious what I mean. I am quite pleased with myself if my voice doesn't tremble at the moment I order the fur coat. Second: the experience. Don't lose sight of that, my friend, the *experience*, the adventure. And—of course—the pleasure of seeing Marija happy: she believes in me. Appreciates me."

"And is that all?"

"What else could you want?" he replied, almost offended. "Besides, this makes it easy for me to endure all the misfortunes in my personal life. I know that I *can* get dressed up whenever I want to, but I walk around in rags. Do you get it? I don't want to, but I can. Thus I have proof of the fact that I am respectable—and powerful!"

"But," it occurred to me, "why doesn't Marija want to wear the fur coat? Did she get wind of some of this?"

"I told her about it."

"You ruined everything by telling her," I pointed out. "Don't you realize? She could even file charges against you."

"That's why I told her about it. So that she would be in a position to accuse me. Maybe she's speaking to a cop at this very moment. I gave her a few days' time to mull it over. What I'm interested in is a completely independent decision on her part."

"Even so, I don't think you should have told her how you came by that fur coat. You could have made something up. For instance . . ."

"I know," said Osip, as crestfallen as a child. "I don't know how to tell a lie. See—I'm incapable of lying when I love someone. I was almost weeping when I urged her not to ask me where I got the fur coat, because I just can't lie, but she was obstinate. Finally I admitted everything to her. But earlier I had resolved to punish her. I would saddle her conscience with both the coat and me."

"Isn't that cruel?" I asked.

"So anyway—how are you amusing yourself these days?" asked Osip.

"I am writing *The Attic*," I said.

We were walking toward the fortress along the edge of the Danube because Osip had resigned himself to the fact that Marija wasn't going to show up for their date.

"That's bound to be some kind of neo-realism," he said. "Dirty, slobbery children, and laundry strung up in the narrow gaps between the buildings of some suburb, and dockside dives, shit-faced railroad switchmen, hookers . . ."

"There's some of that in it," I responded. "After all, the title itself suggests as much. But it remains a horribly self-centered book . . . Do you want to hear more? I have a few notes with me. (You know, I don't like to leave my papers at the mercy of the rats back in the attic) . . . Billy is too stupid for anything other than 'Let me tell you a story!' But I've always valued your opinion . . ."

"Actually, how is Billy? I haven't heard anything about him in ages."

"I threw him out," I said. "*With great difficulty.*"

"But there was no point in doing that," he replied. "He broke up with Marija, eh?"

"Who knows with him? . . . But let's pop into this place here, so I can read to you from my notes. If that's okay with you."

We sat down in a corner, next to the stove. Then I recalled that I had sat at this same table several years before with Marijana. It had been winter. I remember that well. About four in the afternoon. There wasn't a single person in the pub. Marijana's eyes were misting over. We were drinking cognac. And sneaking kisses.

"Osip, do you remember Marijana? The one with long blonde hair?"

"Yes," said Osip. "I think I remember her. It seems to me that you introduced us one time . . . Why do you ask?"

"We drank gin at this table one winter. She was wearing a black knit sweater with a collar of white silk."

"I don't get it," declared Osip. "Is this a segue into your reading?"

"No. It's just . . . A memory."

"Let me hear these jottings of yours already. I liked what you read aloud to me last time at your place in the attic. But . . . I'm intrigued to see how you'll bring all that business in the attic to its conclusion. Especially what you'll do with Eurydice . . . And with Billy Wiseass. (I'm willing to swear that's Igor!)"

We finished our cognac, and I started reading to him:

97

I listened to invisible trains weeping in the night and to crackly leaves latching onto the hard, frozen earth with their fingernails . . .

"Go on," commanded Osip. "I like the beginning."

Everywhere packs of ravenous, scraggly dogs came out to meet us . . . They would accompany us mutely in large packs. But from time to time they would raise their somber, sad eyes to look at us. They had some sort of strange respect for our noiseless steps, for our embraces.

"I think you've already heard this part," I said. "I'd be better off reading you something from 'Walpurgis Night' . . ."

"No, please don't. That bit is repulsive. Don't you find it truly revolting?"

"That's why I want to read it to you. To see just how repugnant it is. I need a sounding board. Understand? For me there is at the moment no place more revolting than the Bay of Dolphins. I'm sick of magnolias and lutes and farces . . ."

"That," continued Osip, "is because you're going from one extreme to the other. *Isn't life somewhere in between?* Incidentally, perhaps I'm wrong here. I'm judging on the basis of those fragments that you read to me last time at your place in the attic. I liked them all at that moment, but—still—doesn't real life, *realitas,* lie somewhere between your attic and your Walpurgis Night?!"

That evening, after I had parted ways with Osip, I took a stroll through the outlying districts of the city to breathe in a little authentic atmosphere. Along the way I thought about Osip's words. Isn't my novel *The Attic* really just a framework? A framework for what?

Afterward I returned to the attic. I lit a candle and began writing. I was convinced that I wouldn't show this passage to Osip. I wouldn't want him to notice how uncertain I was, how hesitant.

This is what I wrote below the earlier note, which ran:

> *I do not like people who squirm their way out of every situation like earthworms. Without scars or scratches. Comedians.*

Beneath that I had recorded the following a few evenings ago when it became obvious that Eurydice would not be coming back:

> *Agnosceo veteris vestigia flamme.*
> *Enriched by a single scar.*

And then:

> *Today I read in the paper that "Insectomort" is guaranteed to exterminate all types of vermin and rats.*
> *Buy "Insectomort" and dispense with the ornamentation that cockroaches bring.*
> *DETHRONE THE ATTIC!*
> *Warm it up with the sun;*
> *Examine the cracks in the wall in radiant sunshine.*

Right after these notes, I started to write:

Tonight we had a furious storm. The raindrops banged against the windows somewhere on the third floor all night long. When the wind died down, all you could hear was the rain generally pouring down and the raspy coughing of a child whose bed was located somewhere below. That must be the little girl with tuberculosis who plays with her rag dolls on the dark, filthy stairs all day long . . .

ATTIC (III)

I couldn't get to sleep. So I relit the candle and pulled out the little sheets of paper I had used to make *The Attic*. Every time I touched it, the manuscript fell open to the section that I had christened in my mind "Bay of the Dolphins." This passage reminded me of a postcard that I had sent Igor almost a year ago: "Best wishes for a Happy New Year from the Islands of the Coconut Palms." I also remember sending him a "Poem of the Coconut Islands" along with the card. Now I had to decide whether I should include this poem, in the original language of course, in *The Attic*:

> *Tanah airku aman dan makmur*
> *Pulau kelapu jang amat subur*
> *Pulau melati pudjaan bangsa*
> *Sedjak dulu kala*

Melanbai-lambai njiur dipantai
Berbisik-bisik radja k'lana
Memudja pulau nan indah permai
Tanah airku!

"You'll definitely end up including that in *The Attic*," commented Igor when I translated the final stanza for him.

I clearly recall my answer to him:

"I've been thinking about it."

Igor just repeated, "I'm willing to bet that you'll put it in."

The rasping cough and the crying of the child on the fourth floor didn't stop. These sounds were merely overwhelmed from time to time by the rain striking the windows and the muffled bursts of wind. (To spite Igor, I shall not add this poem to the book. That's why I tore it to shreds and chucked it into the straw. That way I'll never be able to include it in *The Attic*.)

Thus unburdened, I abandoned the manuscript. Leaving my candle burning, I stared at the ceiling. Sleep simply would not come. So I got up, draped my army-issue blanket over my shoulders (I slept completely dressed) and tiptoed slowly down the rickety staircase to the ground floor. Was it by any chance pangs of conscience that impelled me to do so?

I struck a match down there and looked around for the tenant register. In the dark frame I saw at first only the flame from the match on the smudged glass . . . Then, as I drew closer, I initially saw only my likeness, the ghost of my likeness. Within that dark frame, which the breath of time had coated, the outlines of my form in the match's trembling flame seemed so hopeless, so selfish, so lost. I suddenly realized, and not without revulsion, that my face was the very thing that had concealed the entire attic, and the whole six-story world, from me until now. Despairing at this thought, I let the match burn my fingers. I didn't even drop it when I felt my stomach knotting in pain. It hurts like hell when the flame burns down to your fingernails.

Then I lit a second match and held it up between myself and the heap of characters waiting to receive the grace of being given form.

GROUND FLOOR

Radev Katarina, Building superintendentBorn1899
Flaker, Anton, engine-fitter1907
Flaker Marija, housewife1911
Flaker Marija, student1932
Flaker Ivan, schoolboy1939
Katić Stevan, railway traffic superintendent1910
Katić Anica, housewife1915
Poparić Djuro, railroad switchman1928
Poparić Stana, office assistant1913
Poparić Ljiljana, schoolgirl1945
Poparić Mašinka, schoolgirl1947
Poparić Jadranka, child1954
Poparić Jadranko, child1954

MEZZANINE

Popov Melanija, typist1934
Avramović Jovan, railroad engineer1926
Avramović Slavica, schoolgirl1949
Avramović Danica, housewife1926
Avramović Goran, elementary school pupil1950
Avramović Mirjana, elementary school pupil1951
Avramović Ljiljana, child1955

SECOND FLOOR

Angelov Kosta, engineer, retired1889
Angelov Smilja, office assistant1900
Kifer Albina, midwife 1918
Žakula Bogdan, tram conductor1900
Žakula Pavle, railway traffic superintendent1930
Žakula Melanija, student at the teachers' academy1935
Solunac Dušan, railway conductor1901
Ilić Tihomir, policeman1931

Once again the match burned my fingertips and I tossed it away nervously. The glowing tip ricocheted off the wall in a small arc and then went out with a brief sizzle. At that point I noticed the dampness and mud that had been spreading over the stairs of late. I wanted to leave, to go back, but from somewhere the wind carried the plaintive howling of a train lost in the night. Soon the clattering of the wheels, now somewhere close by, reached my ears. My God, I thought with a shudder, because of my selfishness I never got around to writing the most beautiful poem of all! The song of trains lost in the night. The ballad of train wheels! And every night I drifted off with that song on my mind . . . The great white trains brought me sleep . . .

Lord, I've been living in that attic as if on another planet!

Have I mentioned anyplace that my attic was close to the train station? No, I didn't say that anywhere. Don't the trains themselves bear a bit of the blame for this situation of mine? Didn't they poison me with vast expanses, stars, and selfishness?

Once again I struck a match and illuminated the fourth floor.

Yes, Alek. Our Mr. Alek. His little daughter has a name like a dream: Sanja.

Kovač Alek, stoker1912

His wife died recently. A year or two ago. I remember the cleaning lady telling me something about it. For a long time they had been unable to have any children, and then the woman went off to a sanatorium and that seemed to have helped or at least that's what people said, but maybe there was another factor involved (but one should never speak ill of the dead), and she gave birth to a daughter, but it "wasn't meant to be" and the woman died after the delivery.

(Kovač Anita, housewife19 . .)

A damp, dark green stain spread across the two vertical lines through the name of the deceased, sucking up the ink.

Ever since then, Uncle Alek has been drinking, and fading away. "He who drinks in silence kills himself in silence," as the cleaning lady said of him. "Such is life. It grabs people by the soul and doesn't let them breathe."

I scanned the register floor by floor.

In the final glow of the match, I cast a quick glance at the listing for the attic and discerned Igor's name at once. (It's high time that I added my own name to the register. Igor might have to face some unpleasantness on my account, otherwise.)

Jurin Igor, student1935

"Billy Wiseass," I said half audibly. "Astronomer. Perpetual student. Student-vagabond. Stargazer. Sleepwalker!"

After my return to the attic:

1) Copy out the list of tenants
2) Make inquiries about each one of them individually with the cleaning lady
3) Buy Sanja some chocolate (with hazelnuts) and oranges
4) Go befriend the tenants
5) *Dismount from this planet.*

SUNDAY; A SUNNY DAY

As I went down the stairs this morning I noticed a rusty weathercock that the wind had toppled into the courtyard overnight.

Outside the entrance I ran into my neighbor Alek.

"How's your little daughter?" I inquired.

"Thanks for asking," he said. "She's better this morning. No doubt she kept you awake last night. You know, in these dilapidated old buildings the walls are so thin they're almost transparent."

He was loaded. His breath reeked of *šljivovica*.

"Not at all," I replied. "I didn't hear a thing. I was pretty tired and drifted right off. The murmur of the rain lulled me to sleep."

"But I saw a light on at your place, around three, and so I thought that you were unable to sleep on account of my little girl. This infernal whooping cough is strangling the kid and the neighborhood alike . . . But, if I may ask, what were you working on all night? You must be studying for your exams!"

"I'm writing *The Attic*," I said by force of habit.

"Nice, nice," he said. "Just don't forget the little people who live downstairs from you . . . And don't ruin your eyesight with the light from that candle. I have a forty-watt lightbulb. I can give it to you. I don't need it."

"Thanks," I said, embarrassed, "but I write by candlelight . . . How can I explain . . . So that I create the right atmosphere. You see? It's like when a blue lightbulb goes on in a train compartment . . ."

"Then write by daylight. You can see the attic and the courtyard better then . . . I don't know if you can get a good look at the garden from your window . . . But I've gotten carried away, and I have to head off to work . . ."

He shook my hand and hurried off.

"Anyway, come by for the lightbulb!" he called my way in the entrance hall. "I'm telling you! This business with the candle . . ."

For a moment I remained standing in front of the building, staring into the windows. The morning sun had already begun to dry the gray, damp walls so that only dark spots remained, from which fine, transparent steam was rising. White laundry, soaked by rain and by sun, waved lazily as it hung on the line stretched between the upper floors of the buildings. Pigeons on the iron balustrade along the balcony vigorously flapped their wings. Somewhere on the fourth floor a child was crying. Then this was overpowered by the singing of a young woman. I tried to determine which window the singing was coming from. The woman sang in a youthful morning voice:

> *You'll never be able to gather*
> *The season's first quinces with me . . .*

Then the fluttering curtain on the fourth floor moved to the side and the woman flung the window open wide. Her upper arms shone in the sunlight and her light-colored chintz blouse allowed her breasts to come into view as she bent forward, reaching for the shutters.

When she caught sight of me, she recoiled and lowered her voice a little. Then she stuck out her tongue at me and pulled the curtain shut again. I watched the folds of the curtain billow, and the only words I could pick out from the rest of the song was: *break of day*.

Suddenly the entire building began to sway on its foundations, just like the curtain. I lowered my eyes, because I sensed that the woman behind the curtain was watching me.

As I walked away, I was able to make out the second part of the song as well:

> *You'll never be able to view*
> *The break of day with me . . .*

BELGRADE
NOVEMBER 1959–MAY 1960

TRANSLATOR'S NOTES

p. 17 *Gnohti saeuton*: This is garbled version of the precept *Gnothi seauton* (Greek), meaning "Know thyself." It was inscribed above the portico of the Temple at Delphi.

p. 23 *from the first arson*: Here Kiš has made a rhyming pun in the Serbian genitive case, using the phrases *prvog hica* (from the first *hitac*, or shot) and *prvog lica* (from the first *lice*, or grammatical person).

p. 43 *You're wearing a new dress*: Starting with this paragraph and continuing for over four pages to the phrase "Adieu, mon prince Carnaval," Kiš is quoting/paraphrasing from the 1934 novel *The Magic Mountain* by Thomas Mann. See the chapter entitled "Walpurgis Night," especially beginning on page 398 in the most recent English translation by John E. Woods (Knopf, 1995). While Mann writes in a mixture of French and German, Kiš uses French and Serbian. In addition, Kiš does not quote the entire section, just certain substantial passages.

p. 45 *life's orphans*: The Serbian term employed here is *siročad života*, which is indeed best translated as "orphans of life." But in the novel by Mann, the German phrase used in the midst of the long conversation in French is *Sorgenkinder des Lebens* (*Der Zauberberg*, Frankfurt am Main:

Fischer, 1960. p. 309), an expression that admits of many translations. Woods uses the term "problem children" in the quoted translation, but I have deviated from him in this place to better follow Kiš's version. Previous translators of Mann have rendered the phrase as "life's delicate children" or "worry-children of life," while more modern but overly clinical renditions might evoke the idea of "high-needs children." Had Kiš not used a Serbian phrase that is fairly clear, this translator would indeed have concurred with Woods's rendering, as his chosen term allows both spiritual and physical connotations.

p. 57*some secret dream*: An untranslatable play on words. In Serbian, *san* means dream, while *skrit* is the past participle of the verb *skriti*, which means to hide.

p. 61*kakaform*: This may refer to an imported chocolate drink powder from northern Europe, but it might also be another of Kiš's neologisms. In that case the word would seem to be a mixture of the Serbian terms *kloroform*, *kaka*, and *kakao*, signifying chloroform, excrement, and cocoa, respectively. The unpleasant associations are quite plausible given the narrator's attitudes and actions toward the female character in question.

p. 62*But don't get formal with me*: Serbian has two forms of the singular pronoun "you." The informal form (*ti*) is used for close friends, family members, and children, while the formal form (*vi*) is used for adult acquaintances or strangers. A more literal translation of the narrator's statement would be: "But don't say *vi* to me. You can see that I say *ti* to you."

p. 77 *Žilavka*: A famous variety of Balkan wine.

p. 77 *Hosszú lépés*: A Hungarian drink consisting of wine mixed with soda water.

p. 77 *Vugava*: Another famous variety of Balkan wine.

p. 78 *Fruška Gora*: A small mountain range in northern Serbia between Belgrade and the capital of the Vojvodina, Novi Sad.

p. 78 *Dubrovnik Madrigal*: The title of a poem by the beloved Serbian writer Jovan Dučić (1874–1943).

p. 78 *Ohrid*: A large lake on the border of Macedonia and Albania.

p. 78 *Gračanica*: An important Serbian Orthodox monastery in the southern Serbian province of Kosovo, founded in the fourteenth century.

p. 78 *Prince Marko*: Famous character from Serbian (and Balkan) history and folklore, he was known in Serbian as Kraljević Marko. Marko lived in the late fourteenth century and his reputation paints him as a combination of freedom fighter and rogue.

p. 78*Scutari*: A port located in northern Albania, close to the border with Montenegro, this old city figures prominently in Serbian history and legends.

p. 79*Mother Jevrosima*: Prince Marko's mother.

p. 79*Banović Strahinja*: Medieval Serbian leader in the era of the Ottoman takeover (late fourteenth century).

p. 79*Lazar*: Prince Lazar (1329–1389), the leader of the weakened Serbian state who perished at the famous Battle of Kosovo.

p. 79*Vuk Mandušić*: A fierce Serbian warrior in the influential epic *The Mountain Wreath* by Petar Petrović Njegoš (1813–1851).

p. 79*Simonida*: "Simonida" is a poem by the highly regarded Serbian writer Milan Rakić (1876–1938).

p. 79*Egg of Columbus*: An expression referring to a difficult puzzle with a simple solution. Kiš could be making a link to the Serbian-American inventor Nikola Tesla, who called his presentation on electricity by this name at the Chicago World's Fair in 1893.

p. 94 *giving away furs*: More wordplay. The narrator uses the words *bunda* and *bundeva*, so that a literal translation of the sentence would read: "But, how is it that you are giving out furs like they were pumpkins?"

PETROS ABATZOGLOU, *What Does Mrs. Freeman Want?*
MICHAL AJVAZ, *The Golden Age.*
   The Other City.
PIERRE ALBERT-BIROT, *Grabinoulor.*
YUZ ALESHKOVSKY, *Kangaroo.*
FELIPE ALFAU, *Chromos.*
   Locos.
JOÃO ALMINO, *The Book of Emotions.*
IVAN ÂNGELO, *The Celebration.*
   The Tower of Glass.
DAVID ANTIN, *Talking.*
ANTÓNIO LOBO ANTUNES, *Knowledge of Hell.*
   The Splendor of Portugal.
ALAIN ARIAS-MISSON, *Theatre of Incest.*
IFTIKHAR ARIF AND WAQAS KHWAJA, EDS.,
   Modern Poetry of Pakistan.
JOHN ASHBERY AND JAMES SCHUYLER,
   A Nest of Ninnies.
ROBERT ASHLEY, *Perfect Lives.*
GABRIELA AVIGUR-ROTEM, *Heatwave
   and Crazy Birds.*
HEIMRAD BÄCKER, *transcript.*
DJUNA BARNES, *Ladies Almanack.*
   Ryder.
JOHN BARTH, *LETTERS.*
   Sabbatical.
DONALD BARTHELME, *The King.*
   Paradise.
SVETISLAV BASARA, *Chinese Letter.*
MIQUEL BAUÇÀ, *The Siege in the Room.*
RENÉ BELLETTO, *Dying.*
MAREK BIEŃCZYK, *Transparency.*
MARK BINELLI, *Sacco and Vanzetti
   Must Die!*
ANDREI BITOV, *Pushkin House.*
ANDREJ BLATNIK, *You Do Understand.*
LOUIS PAUL BOON, *Chapel Road.*
   My Little War.
   Summer in Termuren.
ROGER BOYLAN, *Killoyle.*
IGNÁCIO DE LOYOLA BRANDÃO,
   Anonymous Celebrity.
   The Good-Bye Angel.
   Teeth under the Sun.
   Zero.
BONNIE BREMSER, *Troia: Mexican Memoirs.*
CHRISTINE BROOKE-ROSE, *Amalgamemnon.*
BRIGID BROPHY, *In Transit.*
MEREDITH BROSNAN, *Mr. Dynamite.*
GERALD L. BRUNS, *Modern Poetry and
   the Idea of Language.*
EVGENY BUNIMOVICH AND J. KATES, EDS.,
   *Contemporary Russian Poetry:
   An Anthology.*
GABRIELLE BURTON, *Heartbreak Hotel.*
MICHEL BUTOR, *Degrees.*
   Mobile.
   Portrait of the Artist as a Young Ape.
G. CABRERA INFANTE, *Infante's Inferno.*
   Three Trapped Tigers.
JULIETA CAMPOS,
   The Fear of Losing Eurydice.
ANNE CARSON, *Eros the Bittersweet.*
ORLY CASTEL-BLOOM, *Dolly City.*
CAMILO JOSÉ CELA, *Christ versus Arizona.*
   The Family of Pascual Duarte.
   The Hive.
LOUIS-FERDINAND CÉLINE, *Castle to Castle.*
   Conversations with Professor Y.
   London Bridge.

Normance.
North.
Rigadoon.
MARIE CHAIX, *The Laurels of Lake Constance.*
HUGO CHARTERIS, *The Tide Is Right.*
JEROME CHARYN, *The Tar Baby.*
ERIC CHEVILLARD, *Demolishing Nisard.*
LUIS CHITARRONI, *The No Variations.*
MARC CHOLODENKO, *Mordechai Schamz.*
JOSHUA COHEN, *Witz.*
EMILY HOLMES COLEMAN, *The Shutter
   of Snow.*
ROBERT COOVER, *A Night at the Movies.*
STANLEY CRAWFORD, *Log of the S.S. The
   Mrs Unguentine.*
   Some Instructions to My Wife.
ROBERT CREELEY, *Collected Prose.*
RENÉ CREVEL, *Putting My Foot in It.*
RALPH CUSACK, *Cadenza.*
SUSAN DAITCH, *L.C.*
   Storytown.
NICHOLAS DELBANCO, *The Count of Concord.*
   Sherbrookes.
NIGEL DENNIS, *Cards of Identity.*
PETER DIMOCK, *A Short Rhetoric for
   Leaving the Family.*
ARIEL DORFMAN, *Konfidenz.*
COLEMAN DOWELL,
   The Houses of Children.
   Island People.
   Too Much Flesh and Jabez.
ARKADII DRAGOMOSHCHENKO, *Dust.*
RIKKI DUCORNET, *The Complete
   Butcher's Tales.*
   The Fountains of Neptune.
   The Jade Cabinet.
   The One Marvelous Thing.
   Phosphor in Dreamland.
   The Stain.
   The Word "Desire."
WILLIAM EASTLAKE, *The Bamboo Bed.*
   Castle Keep.
   Lyric of the Circle Heart.
JEAN ECHENOZ, *Chopin's Move.*
STANLEY ELKIN, *A Bad Man.*
   Boswell: A Modern Comedy.
   *Criers and Kibitzers, Kibitzers
   and Criers.*
   The Dick Gibson Show.
   The Franchiser.
   George Mills.
   The Living End.
   The MacGuffin.
   The Magic Kingdom.
   Mrs. Ted Bliss.
   The Rabbi of Lud.
   Van Gogh's Room at Arles.
FRANÇOIS EMMANUEL, *Invitation to a
   Voyage.*
ANNIE ERNAUX, *Cleaned Out.*
SALVADOR ESPRIU, *Ariadne in the
   Grotesque Labyrinth.*
LAUREN FAIRBANKS, *Muzzle Thyself.*
   Sister Carrie.
LESLIE A. FIEDLER, *Love and Death in
   the American Novel.*
JUAN FILLOY, *Faction.*
   Op Oloop.
ANDY FITCH, *Pop Poetics.*
GUSTAVE FLAUBERT, *Bouvard and Pécuchet.*
KASS FLEISHER, *Talking out of School.*

FORD MADOX FORD,
The March of Literature.
JON FOSSE, *Aliss at the Fire.*
Melancholy.
MAX FRISCH, *I'm Not Stiller.*
Man in the Holocene.
CARLOS FUENTES, *Christopher Unborn.*
Distant Relations.
Terra Nostra.
Vlad.
Where the Air Is Clear.
TAKEHIKO FUKUNAGA, *Flowers of Grass.*
WILLIAM GADDIS, *J R.*
The Recognitions.
JANICE GALLOWAY, *Foreign Parts.*
The Trick Is to Keep Breathing.
WILLIAM H. GASS, *Cartesian Sonata
and Other Novellas.*
Finding a Form.
A Temple of Texts.
The Tunnel.
Willie Masters' Lonesome Wife.
GÉRARD GAVARRY, *Hoppla! 1 2 3.*
Making a Novel.
ETIENNE GILSON,
The Arts of the Beautiful.
Forms and Substances in the Arts.
C. S. GISCOMBE, *Giscome Road.*
Here.
Prairie Style.
DOUGLAS GLOVER, *Bad News of the Heart.*
The Enamoured Knight.
WITOLD GOMBROWICZ,
A Kind of Testament.
PAULO EMÍLIO SALES GOMES, *P's Three
Women.*
KAREN ELIZABETH GORDON, *The Red Shoes.*
GEORGI GOSPODINOV, *Natural Novel.*
JUAN GOYTISOLO, *Count Julian.*
Exiled from Almost Everywhere.
Juan the Landless.
Makbara.
Marks of Identity.
PATRICK GRAINVILLE, *The Cave of Heaven.*
HENRY GREEN, *Back.*
Blindness.
Concluding.
Doting.
Nothing.
JACK GREEN, *Fire the Bastards!*
JIŘÍ GRUŠA, *The Questionnaire.*
GABRIEL GUDDING,
Rhode Island Notebook.
MELA HARTWIG, *Am I a Redundant
Human Being?*
JOHN HAWKES, *The Passion Artist.*
Whistlejacket.
ELIZABETH HEIGHWAY, ED., *Contemporary
Georgian Fiction.*
ALEKSANDAR HEMON, ED.,
Best European Fiction.
AIDAN HIGGINS, *Balcony of Europe.*
A Bestiary.
Blind Man's Bluff.
Bornholm Night-Ferry.
Darkling Plain: Texts for the Air.
Flotsam and Jetsam.
Langrishe, Go Down.
Scenes from a Receding Past.
Windy Arbours.
KEIZO HINO, *Isle of Dreams.*
KAZUSHI HOSAKA, *Plainsong.*

ALDOUS HUXLEY, *Antic Hay.*
Crome Yellow.
Point Counter Point.
Those Barren Leaves.
Time Must Have a Stop.
NAOYUKI II, *The Shadow of a Blue Cat.*
MIKHAIL IOSSEL AND JEFF PARKER, EDS.,
*Amerika: Russian Writers View the
United States.*
DRAGO JANČAR, *The Galley Slave.*
GERT JONKE, *The Distant Sound.*
Geometric Regional Novel.
Homage to Czerny.
The System of Vienna.
JACQUES JOUET, *Mountain R.*
Savage.
Upstaged.
CHARLES JULIET, *Conversations with
Samuel Beckett and Bram van
Velde.*
MIEKO KANAI, *The Word Book.*
YORAM KANIUK, *Life on Sandpaper.*
HUGH KENNER, *The Counterfeiters.*
*Flaubert, Joyce and Beckett:
The Stoic Comedians.*
Joyce's Voices.
DANILO KIŠ, *The Attic.*
Garden, Ashes.
The Lute and the Scars
Psalm 44.
A Tomb for Boris Davidovich.
ANITA KONKKA, *A Fool's Paradise.*
GEORGE KONRÁD, *The City Builder.*
TADEUSZ KONWICKI, *A Minor Apocalypse.*
The Polish Complex.
MENIS KOUMANDAREAS, *Koula.*
ELAINE KRAF, *The Princess of 72nd Street.*
JIM KRUSOE, *Iceland.*
AYŞE KULIN, *Farewell: A Mansion in
Occupied Istanbul.*
EWA KURYLUK, *Century 21.*
EMILIO LASCANO TEGUI, *On Elegance
While Sleeping.*
ERIC LAURRENT, *Do Not Touch.*
HERVÉ LE TELLIER, *The Sextine Chapel.*
*A Thousand Pearls (for a Thousand
Pennies)*
VIOLETTE LEDUC, *La Bâtarde.*
EDOUARD LEVÉ, *Autoportrait.*
Suicide.
MARIO LEVI, *Istanbul Was a Fairy Tale.*
SUZANNE JILL LEVINE, *The Subversive
Scribe: Translating Latin
American Fiction.*
DEBORAH LEVY, *Billy and Girl.*
*Pillow Talk in Europe and Other
Places.*
JOSÉ LEZAMA LIMA, *Paradiso.*
ROSA LIKSOM, *Dark Paradise.*
OSMAN LINS, *Avalovara.*
The Queen of the Prisons of Greece.
ALF MAC LOCHLAINN,
The Corpus in the Library.
Out of Focus.
RON LOEWINSOHN, *Magnetic Field(s).*
MINA LOY, *Stories and Essays of Mina Loy.*
BRIAN LYNCH, *The Winner of Sorrow.*
D. KEITH MANO, *Take Five.*
MICHELINE AHARONIAN MARCOM,
The Mirror in the Well.
BEN MARCUS,
The Age of Wire and String.

WALLACE MARKFIELD,
Teitlebaum's Window.
To an Early Grave.
DAVID MARKSON, *Reader's Block.*
Springer's Progress.
Wittgenstein's Mistress.
CAROLE MASO, *AVA.*
LADISLAV MATEJKA AND KRYSTYNA
POMORSKA, EDS.,
Readings in Russian Poetics:
Formalist and Structuralist Views.
HARRY MATHEWS,
The Case of the Persevering Maltese:
Collected Essays.
Cigarettes.
The Conversions.
The Human Country: New and
Collected Stories.
The Journalist.
My Life in CIA.
Singular Pleasures.
The Sinking of the Odradek
Stadium.
Tlooth.
20 Lines a Day.
JOSEPH MCELROY,
Night Soul and Other Stories.
THOMAS MCGONIGLE,
Going to Patchogue.
ROBERT L. MCLAUGHLIN, ED., *Innovations:*
An Anthology of Modern &
Contemporary Fiction.
ABDELWAHAB MEDDEB, *Talismano.*
GERHARD MEIER, *Isle of the Dead.*
HERMAN MELVILLE, *The Confidence-Man.*
AMANDA MICHALOPOULOU, *I'd Like.*
STEVEN MILLHAUSER, *The Barnum Museum.*
In the Penny Arcade.
RALPH J. MILLS, JR., *Essays on Poetry.*
MOMUS, *The Book of Jokes.*
CHRISTINE MONTALBETTI, *The Origin of Man.*
Western.
OLIVE MOORE, *Spleen.*
NICHOLAS MOSLEY, *Accident.*
Assassins.
Catastrophe Practice.
Children of Darkness and Light.
Experience and Religion.
A Garden of Trees.
God's Hazard.
The Hesperides Tree.
Hopeful Monsters.
Imago Bird.
Impossible Object.
Inventing God.
Judith.
Look at the Dark.
Natalie Natalia.
Paradoxes of Peace.
Serpent.
Time at War.
The Uses of Slime Mould:
Essays of Four Decades.
WARREN MOTTE,
Fables of the Novel: French Fiction
since 1990.
Fiction Now: The French Novel in
the 21st Century.
Oulipo: A Primer of Potential
Literature.
GERALD MURNANE, *Barley Patch.*
Inland.

YVES NAVARRE, *Our Share of Time.*
Sweet Tooth.
DOROTHY NELSON, *In Night's City.*
Tar and Feathers.
ESHKOL NEVO, *Homesick.*
WILFRIDO D. NOLLEDO, *But for the Lovers.*
FLANN O'BRIEN, *At Swim-Two-Birds.*
At War.
The Best of Myles.
The Dalkey Archive.
Further Cuttings.
The Hard Life.
The Poor Mouth.
The Third Policeman.
CLAUDE OLLIER, *The Mise-en-Scène.*
Wert and the Life Without End.
GIOVANNI ORELLI, *Walaschek's Dream.*
PATRIK OUŘEDNÍK, *Europeana.*
The Opportune Moment, 1855.
BORIS PAHOR, *Necropolis.*
FERNANDO DEL PASO, *News from the Empire.*
Palinuro of Mexico.
ROBERT PINGET, *The Inquisitory.*
Mahu or The Material.
Trio.
A. G. PORTA, *The No World Concerto.*
MANUEL PUIG, *Betrayed by Rita Hayworth.*
The Buenos Aires Affair.
Heartbreak Tango.
RAYMOND QUENEAU, *The Last Days.*
Odile.
Pierrot Mon Ami.
Saint Glinglin.
ANN QUIN, *Berg.*
Passages.
Three.
Tripticks.
ISHMAEL REED, *The Free-Lance Pallbearers.*
The Last Days of Louisiana Red.
Ishmael Reed: The Plays.
Juice!
Reckless Eyeballing.
The Terrible Threes.
The Terrible Twos.
Yellow Back Radio Broke-Down.
JASIA REICHARDT, *15 Journeys Warsaw*
to London.
NOËLLE REVAZ, *With the Animals.*
JOÃO UBALDO RIBEIRO, *House of the*
Fortunate Buddhas.
JEAN RICARDOU, *Place Names.*
RAINER MARIA RILKE, *The Notebooks of*
Malte Laurids Brigge.
JULIÁN RÍOS, *The House of Ulysses.*
Larva: A Midsummer Night's Babel.
Poundemonium.
Procession of Shadows.
AUGUSTO ROA BASTOS, *I the Supreme.*
DANIËL ROBBERECHTS, *Arriving in Avignon.*
JEAN ROLIN, *The Explosion of the*
Radiator Hose.
OLIVIER ROLIN, *Hotel Crystal.*
ALIX CLEO ROUBAUD, *Alix's Journal.*
JACQUES ROUBAUD, *The Form of a*
City Changes Faster, Alas, Than
the Human Heart.
The Great Fire of London.
Hortense in Exile.
Hortense Is Abducted.
The Loop.
Mathematics:
The Plurality of Worlds of Lewis.